I0690023

CITIZEN SECOND CLASS

Apocalypse Next

ROBERT CHAZZ CHUTE

Citizen Second Class

Copyright © 2019 by Robert Chazz Chute

All rights reserved.

No part of this book may be reproduced in any form or by any electronic or mechanical means, including information storage and retrieval systems, without written permission from the author, except for the use of brief quotations in a book review.

Please address media and all rights inquiries to expartepress@gmail.com.

ISBN (paperback) 978-1-927607-67-1
ISBN (Ebook) 978-1-927607-66-4

WHAT READERS SAY ABOUT ROBERT'S WORK

Chute sucks you in from word one and pulls you down his post-apocalyptic rabbit hole! You will sleep with the lights on, covers pulled over your head and dust off the old teddy bear for comfort. Chazz ranks among the top tier of our generation's storytellers. - Alex Kimmell, Author of *The Key to Everything*

Robert Chazz Chute is such a skilled spinner of tales that the reader is more than willing to suspend any possible disbelief to go along for the ride. - David Pandolfe, author of *Jump When Ready*

It's not very often one finds a writer with such a dark side that has such a great sense of humor. - Glenn Roberts, Amazon reviewer

The author has a definite talent with words and ideas. ~ Love to Read!, Amazon reviewer

His words lift and dance off the page, bringing the story to life. ~ Kindle Customer, Amazon reviewer

The world-building is horrifically well done with twists and turns and deceit around every corner. ~ Wanda, Amazon reviewer

RCC blends characters' beliefs & worries concerning society's failures, plus vivid action scenes skillfully. ~ RMerkl, Amazon Reviewer
Nothing but sheer exhaustion could tear my eyes from the captivating dance of words choreographed by Robert Chazz Chute. ~ Halph Staph, Amazon reviewer

Wonderful action constantly holds your interest. ~ Sharon Finn, Amazon reviewer

The complexity and attention to detail throughout absolutely blow me away. ~ Kindle customer, Amazon Reviewer

Very few authors impress me with their actual writing style, it's usually always about the story. But this author paints such beautiful vivid pictures with words that I found myself not only enjoying the story but enjoying the way the words created images in my mind. I know that sounds corny, but it is true. - B.H., Amazon reviewer

Chute gives us story worthy of Stephen King. A read both thoughtful and fun. - Linda Beer Johnson, Amazon reviewer

The author does an excellent job building the characters and getting you invested and involved. - Michele L. Hebert, Amazon reviewer

I just can't say in words what a powerful author this is! - Delinda L. Calkins, Amazon reviewer

Robert Chazz Chute writes so skillfully as to make the supernatural seem perfectly logical - and terrifying! There are twists, turns and surprises galore. You will be glad you bought this book - until you lose sleep because you can't put it down. - johligo, Amazon reviewer

When I want to read apocalyptic books or zombie stories, those books have to also be extremely well-written and something that I could recommend with zeal and confidence to everyone I know. Robert Chazz Chute's books are exactly that. - Mazie Lane, Amazon reviewer

He makes the stuff that is obviously fiction, believable. - W. Nickels,
Amazon reviewer

I am a lover of paranormal, dystopian novels and depth of story as well
as intelligence in writing style, and Robert has it all. Humor, wit,
depth, intelligence and an awesome way with words/writing. - Amazon
Customer, Amazon reviewer

Dedicated to the children of Flint,
unwilling emblems of a criminal lack of empathy,
lasting symbols of the rot in the pipes.
That corruption is everywhere and
it has to stop.

EPIGRAPH

"Write hard and clear about what hurts."
- Ernest Hemingway

"The American dream is dead."
- Donald J. Trump

"At the base of every great fortune there is a great crime."
- Balzac

"When the rich rob the poor, it's called business.
When the poor fight back, it's called violence."
- Mark Twain

"When we revolt it's not for a particular culture. We revolt simply
because, for many reasons, we can no longer breathe."
-Frantz Fanon

CHAPTER ONE

The last time my whole family was together, my mother still had both legs and Grammy still remembered we didn't have a president anymore. The pictures, taken in the soft light of early morning, show my sister and my parents standing together, looking sharp in their uniforms. In our old gray dresses, Grammy and I seem washed out, present but somehow incomplete, diluted. By the time the sun rose to a hard glare, the ones in uniform were on their way to their posts, answering the call of duty. I was left to care for my grandmother.

"They're off to close the distance between ought and is," Grammy said. "Good luck to 'em, cuz, good God, that's a need! All our lives we're told to make stacks and save wads and now we can't even make change. Sometimes life feels like we're set to fight a forest fire with nothing but a water pistol and a box o' dry crackers, dudn't it?"

She put her thin stick of an arm around my shoulder and said, "And here you are, stuck in the sticks with an old lady to watch out for, makin' sure I don't wander off. Won't exactly be your halcyon days, huh? You feel left behind? Or left out? You could stick me on an ice floe, maybe."

"I don't think there are any ice floes left, Grammy."

She chuckled. "Looks like you're stuck, then."

I didn't mind. I loved her and I didn't want to be a part of any battles. However, in the war for the future, we are all drafted.

I thought I was relatively safe growing up in a little town in Georgia. However, the tendrils of conflict wound their way everywhere, even to our tiny part of the world. I had to leave my little town of Campbellford. If we were to survive, we had to take drastic action.

"They say this winter will be the warmest yet." Grammy fanned herself on her rocking chair on the front porch. She used to rock for hours out there. Grammy didn't have the energy to rock in her chair anymore. She sat still, listened to the quiet and complained that her nightly concert of frogs and crickets was gone. The marsh had dried up.

"Lots of traffic used to come through Campbellford on their way to some damn place, to and fro. By times one or two of those automatic trucks still blows past, just ugly gray boxes they are, all speeding, all dangerous and never stopping around here. Not a single driver in them. That used to be our number one job by population: drivin' truck and deliverin' things hither and thither. Now that there's more trucks barrelin' up and down the roads and no drivers, I think that's why we got stuck with all this extreme weather. The air, Kismet! It's so darn *close*."

"Humid, you mean?"

"The air never used to be so close!"

"I know. The humidity makes my hair all frizzy."

"You have quite a mop on you, more of a hair don't that a hairdo. Get the scissors, I'll give you a trim."

Grammy wasn't dangerous but I wasn't about to hand her scissors. Her creeping dementia had already made me elder-proof the house. If she cut my hair, I'd worry she might not stop cutting when she got to my ears.

"I'll get you your hand fan to keep the heat at bay," I said.

"I got no energy to be wavin' that thing at myself all day."

"Then I'll fan you."

"I don't pay with anything but smiles and a nod. You goin' out lookin' for a job tomorrow?"

She said tomorrow like *tomorrah*. I once asked her where she got her expressions.

"Wasn't always stuck in a rocking chair in this little town. My family lived on turd stew sometimes but we used to move all over and live all over. I talk same as I did when I was your age. When I was young, so was the world. The world's as old as me now and lookin' no better. I don't care for it."

"You look lovely, Grammy."

"My grandmother would have called that statement a bunch of horsefeathers."

"What would you say?"

"I say, break all the mirrors!"

I ignored her and ducked into the house for a moment. "I can't find the fan!" I called. "Where'd you put it?"

By the time I returned she'd forgotten what I went searching for. "Ah! A fan," she said. "Can't keep the stink off but maybe we can wave it downwind. Good idea."

She gave me a smile and a nod as I fanned her. It was payment enough, but where memory failed, habits took over. She didn't leave her favorite topics alone for long. Whenever she was annoyed, she would bring up my lack of employment. I helped out at the town's food bank but the work wasn't steady and paid in tins of fake fish.

"Maybe there are still things to do like changing tires on those robot trucks, huh?"

"I think the robots pretty much take care of the robots," I replied.

"Incestuous business," she said. "Or is that ... what's the word?"

"Nepotism?"

The way her eyebrows knitted together, I suspected that was a word that was now lost to her vocabulary.

"All you got is odd jobs, Kismet."

"All the jobs are odd now. It's not like when you were young and Jesus was still a carpenter running his own business."

"Ain't that so," she said. "Even his business went bad. Nobody's paying our savior any attention anymore. Everybody needs Jesus but we're past the point of no return, aren't we?"

"It's not that bad. Not quite yet, anyway."

"Isn't it? You only say that because you don't remember how it was before."

"Then I guess I'm lucky. When you don't know how good it was, you can't miss it."

I didn't know how much worse things could get. Not then. We called it the Slow Apocalypse because the troubles had taken so long to mount. The future was a dark and looming cloud, but its shadow had taken over the landscape for so long, we were more fatigued than frightened.

The collapse started slow, like when the swamp and the jobs dried up at the same time. Lots of people's jobs were going away and who's really going to miss a swamp? With the frogs dead and the crickets gone to wherever crickets go, the nights were quieter. When the power rationing began, we told ourselves that was just the way it was and, with not a light in sight all the way to Atlanta, the stars seemed brighter.

"No shine from the humankind," Grammy marveled. "No light to compete with the Milky Way. I haven't seen the night sky so well since my eyes were good and I was younger than you."

The cost of chicken was the first thing I really noticed. Grammy used to prepare chicken breasts for me, skin off and baked not fried. It was supposed to be healthier that way, for those who cared, for those who still clung to the idea that a longer life was important.

"I prefer the old way, Southern done, fried up with lots of grease," Grammy told me, "but we gotta keep you strong and healthy for what's ahead."

"What's ahead?" I asked.

"A whole lot less than what's behind."

Then Grammy stopped buying chicken. The price climbed too high. "We used to keep chickens in the yard back in Raleigh. We were poor but we never went hungry. Mostly we lived off the eggs but even the eggs are getting up there."

"Up where?"

"Up where we don't belong, with the rich folks."

The pig fever epidemic had hit hard the first fall that Daddy, Mama and Sissy were away. China slaughtered almost all of them.

"They got a few pigs left in a special zoo underground somewhere," Grammy said. "Keepin' 'em around so's they don't go extinct, preserving the DNA so they can bring 'em back someday. If that grand resurrection happens, it'll be long after my day. Too bad. My mother used to make me bacon on grilled cheese when I came home from school each day. I used to love head cheese and trotter stew."

"Trotter stew?" I made a face and she laughed. Later, when all was quiet and I had some time to think, I wondered if Grammy was trying to turn my stomach on purpose, maybe to make me miss bacon less. The veggie bacon from the food bank wasn't quite the same.

Then, when the embargoes began, the grocery store changed. There was still stuff on the shelves but nothing was fresh. "Food all tastes the same now," Grammy complained, "as if it's the same crap in different molds, processed up the wazoo and bland. Even the packaging is bland now. They don't even have to bother with making the labels colorful and pretty anymore. You get what you get and you're told to be grateful. Unless it's the outhouse, I forget why I walked into a room these days. My memory of better days is still good, though. That's kind of cruel isn't it? Makes you think God got tired of us and wandered away to work on more interesting projects."

A little weary of her whining, I reminded her there was a war on.

"Always was, always will be," Grammy spat. "And when do you think your mother, father and Sissy will get back from it? You listen to the news. How we doin'?"

"They say we're winning." Even as I said it, no strength bolstered my words. "Let it alone, Grammy."

I missed my parents. Rich and Kacy Beatriz were both Army infantry.

"We met while we were on containment duty," Mama told us. "I looked over and here was this big man with a jaw like a steam shovel and I thought, 'Now that's a man.' Rich looked over at me and our eyes met. We knew right away, like we'd been spending our lives waiting for the other one to show up."

Mama and Daddy were married by an Army chaplain in a tent on the side of a hill looking out at Alcatraz. They had one night of leave, conceived Sissy and went right back to manning the barriers the next morning.

I loved that story. Despite the demands of their work, my parents saw each other's best selves. Bad times don't always build heroes but they met at a time when they could still believe in their mission to protect our country.

"Your daddy and the propapundits say good times are comin' back," Grammy said. "They're taking their damn time and mighta gotten lost along the way. I wonder where they all are right now."

"Leave it alone, Grammy. They'll be back when they can come back."

"You gonna look for a job, Kismet?"

"Leave it alone, Grammy."

My sister found work following my parents into the service.

"Smart as a whip, that girl," Grammy told me. "But too good for this place, always had her eye on the horizon. Your sister always wanted to be somewhere else even though all places are pretty much the same."

Sissy was born Susan. She got her new moniker after I was born. I couldn't pronounce her name properly at first and Sissy stuck.

She joined the Air Force. She wanted to take the training in New Chicago to be a doctor. They call it New Chicago but they really mean North Chicago. Chicago officially became two cities but they say it was always two cities, anyway.

Late at night when it was too hot to sleep, I'd sit in Grammy's rocker and watch for meteors. My grandmother could still name all the constellations but, even without light pollution, she couldn't see the stars very well, anymore. The diabetes got to her eyes.

Grammy's memory was getting worse and so was her outlook. "Some nights I lay in bed in the heat and I think one of them big rocks will come down from outer space and put us out of our misery, put us down like a dog. But it ain't all over. You got some livin' to do yet. Don't you worry. There's still time for you."

She told me the same thing many times. Even though the news was new to her each time, I sensed less and less conviction.

After she was down for the night, I'd sit out on the porch and wonder how much time there was left and how I should spend it. Time used to be malleable. It could stretch and compress and play tricks. Now it seemed a short and tired thing. Just like our money, it was limited, easy to spend and almost as dried up as the swamp.

It's true you don't miss what you never had but I did remember the noise from the frogs and crickets. It was a wild thrum, call and response, a choir whose church was nature. I liked the quiet but too much silence can get to a person. You think you like something and then you get too much of it.

That was how I felt when I got the encrypted message from my sister. My bracelet lit my face, the only electronic glow for miles. Tears slipped down my cheeks as I read and reread her plea. I hadn't heard from her in a long time and she'd set the note to be delivered months after it was written. She made it clear I was needed, that I was the only one she could trust for the task she'd set. My instructions were short and precise. I had to leave Grammy behind to answer my own call of duty.

I memorized the message and erased it. Then I walked down the road in the dark and knocked on my closest neighbor's door. Lisa Gott was at her kitchen table reading by an oil lamp. I told her what I needed, what Grammy needed to know and what she didn't need to know.

Lisa's husband Buddy was away, stationed in Vancouver, Washington. She understood and didn't hesitate to agree to help.

I needed her to say yes but, to be polite, I asked, "You're sure? The refrigerator isn't even hooked up anymore but Grammy keeps putting things in it. If she runs out of clothes in her bedroom, sometimes that's where you'll find them."

"Kismet, after what you did for this town, for Buddy and me?"

"I took no pleasure in that — "

"It was necessary. You came through for all of us. You'll never hear no from me."

The next morning, I assured Grammy all would be well in my absence. "Lisa will check in on you. The money from Daddy and Mama will keep coming. You always said the wars will never end so you can depend on the money. If you're short, Lisa can help out with rations from the food bank."

"You gonna leave a blind old woman to her own self just like that, huh? Just like Sissy and your father. Like your mother, you've got that wanderlust. That's the trouble."

"Grammy, I love you, but you keep telling me I need a job. You tell me that every day. It's time I looked where the jobs are. That means going farther down the road."

"Well, bless us and bless you," Grammy said sourly. "You know the difference between a hot clammy night you can't sleep and a sweaty sultry summer night, Kismet?" Grammy asked. "Your mood and your company. You want to survive in this world, you need an umbrella for your troubles. Go into Atlanta and see if y'all can find the right people to keep you safe."

As I walked down the dusty road headed south past abandoned farms and empty buildings, ragged yellow ribbons were tied around many of the trees. It seemed everyone from the area had at least one family member in the military.

I pushed that thought away and focused on breathing and walking, just like Mama taught me. I told myself I was on an adventure. Bad times can make heroes. I wanted to believe that. I wanted to make it true.

CHAPTER TWO

The road south to Atlanta was mostly quiet and abandoned. I heard birds in the distance but I missed the rattling alarm of squirrels. In the last year or so, most of them had been hunted close to extinction. One squirrel didn't feed many but several in a stew could last a couple of days if rationed properly.

I walked for a couple of hours before I hit the first checkpoint. Three guardsmen in camouflage waited at a T-junction in a beat-up white SUV. Parked in front of a shuttered convenience store, their camo served no function other than to intimidate. I had two knives on me I didn't want to lose and I thought I might lose them if they searched me. I considered turning into the woods but they'd already spotted me. If I made them chase me, I could get arrested or worse. I decided to play it cool.

A pair of sleepy guardsmen sat side-by-side on the truck's tailgate. Grizzled and worn, I noticed they were both amputees, one with one leg and the other with none. Their prosthetic legs clacked together a little as they passed a thermos back and forth.

I'd seen plenty of veterans with metal legs by then. However, the fact that the two were together seemed an odd detail. I wondered, *Is this real? Am I hallucinating from hunger and dehydration already?*

The third guard was a woman in an exoskeleton. She had all her limbs but the gear allowed her to stand for long periods without expending energy. She hefted her rifle and gave me a hard look.

I took that as my cue to come to a stop. "Good morning to you."

She didn't reply immediately and I guessed she was waiting for the scanner in her goggles to complete its facial-recognition run.

Impatient to get going before the heat of the day forced me to find shade, I offered, "Hello?"

"Kismet Beatriz?"

"Yes?"

"State your business."

"Headed to Atlanta for work."

The guard made a face. "What work?"

"I don't know yet. I gotta go find it."

"There's no work in Atlanta."

"Maybe so. There's even less work around here."

One of the guards on the back of the truck cackled. I wasn't sure if he was laughing at me or at her. I suspected the thermos contained something stronger than soup.

"Lotta people coming the other way," the woman told me. "A column of illegals passed by here last night."

"Oh? I didn't see anyone."

"They always say they're looking for work, too."

"I wouldn't know about that. I haven't seen anyone this morning except for a fox, some birds and a couple of feral cats."

"You hear about the protests?"

The way she asked, the question almost sounded like she was sharing gossip. I knew better. My father had always been clear about the Citizen Security and Safety Force. "They may wear roughly the same uniform but they are not your friends. Never let *your* guard down with one of them. They're doing different duty than your mother and me."

"I don't know anything about any protests."

"The Apple-a-Chicks are marching on Washington," she said.

I knew the name. They called their organization the Organization of Appalachian Women for Income Equality. The propapundits first called them the OAWIES or OWIES, for a shorter and more dismissive taunt. That name didn't catch on. Apple-a-Chicks polled better with the Select Few so the media switched to the new moniker to mock the movement.

"There are rumors," the guard said. "You heard anything about protest activities down here?"

The idea that there were enough Apple-a-Chicks to stir up trouble in my state seemed as remote as Muslim extremists targeting my little town with a dirty bomb. "In Georgia? Pretty far from the action, aren't we?" I made the mistake of smiling as I answered.

One of the guards sitting on the SUV's tail grumbled, "Trouble's everywhere, girl."

"Protest groups have been linked to our president's assassination," the other added, not looking up.

Though his death was not new, members of the CSS seemed particularly aggrieved by his passing. They never said *the* president. They always said *our* president. Meaning: *not yours.*

The Appalachian women protesters had been implicated in the assassination, but anyone who'd ever criticized him was suspect.

"I've never seen any protesters around here," I said.

"Maybe it wasn't them specifically," the guard in the exoskeleton corrected me. "Maybe it's them and maybe it isn't but don't talk like it matters. A protest group is fertile soil for traitors and terrorists. Disloyal is disloyal, whatever quarter it comes from."

Unlike my grandmother, she must have believed every word uttered by the propapundits.

"Where *you* comin' from, Kismet?" one of the men on the truck asked.

"Campbellford."

"What's there?"

"Not much. It's home. I live with my grandmother."

"You got a job prospect down in Atlanta?"

"Nothing solid, just going to look and see what I can find."

The third guard looked at me with heavily lidded eyes. "Nice pack. Where'd you get it?"

The backpack belonged to my father and I told him so.

The female guard, tall and towering over me in her exo-gear, ordered me to take it off. She tossed it to the pair on the tailgate and they rummaged through my belongings.

"Must not be too busy around here," I said. "Haven't seen a car on the road, either."

"If you're implying we don't have enough to do — "

"I didn't say that."

"You didn't have to." She placed herself between me and the SUV so I couldn't see the men rifle through my bag.

"Where'd your father serve?" the woman asked.

"Lots of places. My parents were out west on a peacekeeping mission. That pack went to the Middle Beast with my father on his first two tours. When you guys dig to the bottom you'll probably find some sand from Afghanistan or Iran. My mother served there, too."

"Your parents are *both* warrior class?"

"My sister, too, yeah. Air Force."

"Why aren't you?"

I felt like I'd already given up too much of myself to them so I just shrugged.

"Uh-huh. That's the problem with you people." She stalked back to the SUV in a few long strides. The weight of her exoskeleton left deep impressions in the macadam. She retrieved my pack and tossed it at my feet.

My underwear was poking out of the top. Embarrassed, I stuffed it back inside. When I picked it up, it felt light. When I looked to the men at the back of the SUV, they grinned and held up several ration packs. "Thanks for the grub, Kismet!"

"You aren't guardsmen. You're thieves."

The woman stepped forward suddenly and used the broadside of her rifle to push me back. "Watch your mouth, girl. You only get to complain when you've sacrificed something."

"I just gave up my rations and some dignity, I guess."

"Maybe you better turn around and head home to your grandmother," one of the men told me. "If you're no use to us, maybe you can do something for her. Or join up! You join up, you become a citizen and you get to vote, so why not? It's what patriots do."

"Thanks for the advice."

"It's free! Take it for what it's worth!" He cackled at me and the other two joined in.

I pulled my pack back on my shoulders and retreated toward home. It's a funny thing about getting pushed around. Before I came upon that checkpoint, I really hadn't given the Apple-a-Chicks much thought. Their protests were far away and seemed irrelevant to me. After being bullied by armed guards, I wanted to know more about the protests. Given the chance, I wanted to join one. Whatever their politics, if the protesters pissed them off, the Apple-a-Chicks were worth my support.

I hadn't joined the warrior class to earn full citizenship. Propapundits were like musicians who only knew two notes: Trust those who lead our great nation, honor the centurions who protect it.

But I'd seen what our leaders and the CSS had done. Coming from a military family, I knew how shallow their reverence for the military really was. Neither my parents nor my sister felt they lived in a world of choice. Except for members of the Select Few, I don't think there were ever many choices.

Grammy was certain our fates were set and we were all doomed. "Trains run on rails," she would say. "They go from here to there and that's it. Trains don't wander off course. People like to think they're different from trains. Mostly, they aren't. Doesn't matter. Everything's off the rails, isn't it?"

I was determined to find a new way forward that didn't end in derailment and disaster. As soon as I was around a corner and out of sight, I doubled back through the woods. I gave the checkpoint a wide berth so they wouldn't scan me on thermo.

Atlanta was a long walk but I still had a filter straw to decontaminate water. I could drink from a creek if and when I found one. The rations were a hard loss but I was used to hunger.

I told myself this was only the beginning of my grand adventure. Grammy would have told me my train was already derailing.

CHAPTER THREE

I didn't have a tent but I had a tarp. The creek beds were dry but it rained hard that night. I used the tarp to funnel rainwater into my mouth. It was a rough night's sleep and it was still raining when I set off the next morning. Though the day started off wet and miserable, by noon, the sun and the heat forced me to shelter under a dead ash tree. I spread the tarp out again to dry it.

A few people wandered by, heading in the direction I'd come. A haggard white woman pushing an empty stroller asked if she could buy some water. I shrugged and told her I had nothing for her. She cursed me and kept going, marching on. I tried to tell her I hadn't seen any water sources except for the rain. The woman turned and spat and I watched her go. She got smaller and smaller until she was a dot and then she was nothing.

An hour later, I spotted a convoy of military trucks rumbling in the same direction. I slipped behind the tree and waited for them to disappear. Would they stop for the woman? What might the CSS demand in return for a bottle of water? I didn't know and didn't want to think about it.

I fell asleep under the dead ash tree and woke with a start, eager to get back on the road to Atlanta while it was light. I gathered my things and, after another hour or so, came upon a larger road. My stomach growled and I felt a little lightheaded. AUTONAV trucks blew past me at full speed. When I came upon a short break in traffic I clambered over a barrier and sprinted to the other side of the highway. Using my bracelet, I tried to get the attention of two AUTONAV buses. They were for citizens only, I guess, because the bus scanner did not register my presence and sped on.

I began to walk, my thumb out. Shortly, a man and a woman in a fancy red sports car stopped to offer me a ride.

The man had a huge head and was jowly, a sure sign of prosperity. "Fat as a tick," Grammy would say. "If he were an inch taller, he'd be perfectly round."

The woman wore thick makeup. The bright red lipstick she had dragged around her mouth to make her lips look bigger reminded me of pictures of clowns. The couple's low-slung car looked like it was built for speed in a way its owners were not. I climbed in the back and we roared off. The fuel was organic, not electric, so I was sure I was in the presence of a member of the Select Few. That meant they had to be bound for Atlanta. I thought my luck had changed.

"I'm Chuck," the driver said. "That's Marjorie."

"I'm his paramour," she giggled.

I wasn't familiar with that word but I deduced she meant that they were a couple. I nodded agreeably. "Thanks for the ride." The seats were so soft I might have fallen asleep if I weren't so hungry. The air conditioning blew cool air over my skin, chilling the sweat. I shivered but I was grateful, too.

"You running away from home?" Chuck asked. "I don't normally see a lot of girls out along the highway alone. You're lucky the CSS didn't pick you up for hitching."

"I'm headed to Atlanta, looking for work."

"Oh, really?" Marjorie looked intrigued. "Young girl, all on her own, on your first big adventure?"

I didn't like the way she looked me up and down. "Just looking for a job, ma'am."

"Ma'am! Ooh, so polite! I like this one, Chuck. You should give her a job!"

Chuck's eyes flicked up into the rearview mirror. He stared at me for a beat longer than seemed wise. He was driving and the car was not in autonomous mode. His was not a threatening look, not exactly. More of an appraisal, as if he was trying to calculate my exact worth to him. I didn't care for Marjorie's smile, either.

I felt lightheaded and a little sick in the back of their car. I closed my eyes for a moment to will the nausea away. *This is real,* I thought. *This is happening. Keep your guard up.*

Daddy was a combat instructor. I wasn't military, but he'd taught me how to defend myself. It wasn't fear that rose through my chest as they drove me south. It was something else I had not felt since the previous spring, the night I confronted Clayton Dobbs.

I pushed that thought away. Lisa and Buddy Gott were grateful for what I did for Campbellford, but I didn't like to think about Dobbs.

"Y'know, you're a little odoriferous, out there in the sun all day," Marjorie said. "We could take you home and give you a bath. Would you like that? Would you like us to give you a bath?"

I had given no thought to defending myself against the three armed guardsmen, especially since one was in an exoskeleton and armed with a rifle. That would have been stupid. However, I was confident I could handle these two. They looked soft and I wore two knives.

One blade was in a sheath at the small of my back. The other was strapped to my left forearm. Both combat knives, black and sharp, were gifts from my parents. They were given to me when I was thirteen, on the day of my first menstruation.

Marjorie who got right to the point. "How far you wanna go with us, girl?"

"Like I said, Atlanta, if you're headed that far."

"No, I mean how far are you willing to go? Chuck and I can take you all the way if you're willing to pay the toll. Are you catching what I'm tossing your way? It's an opportunity." She winked and licked her painted lips lasciviously.

"Or you could just let me out here."

"You eaten lately, honey?" she persisted.

I sighed. My parents had strong ideas about how to hurt people who needed hurting. My sister was more devious. I decided to try

Sissy's brand of tactics. "Chuck? Marjorie? Do you want to hear a story?"

"Chuck and I *love* stories. Do tell!"

"Once upon a time, there was a girl on the run."

"A runaway? Runaways are interesting," Marjorie said.

"Shut up, Marjorie," Chuck ordered. "Let her talk. She doesn't sound like a Mexican, but I like the way she talks."

I ignored his slur and continued breezily. "This girl didn't run away from home. She ran from authorities. They hunted her but she lost herself in the woods. Lots of woods in Georgia. That's where this girl was from."

Chuck's eyes flicked up to look at me in the rearview mirror again. His eyes were wider this time, less sure of himself, less smug.

"This girl wasn't treated well. She always had a perfect memory for every bad thing that happened to her. Lots of bad people everywhere and she ran into one or two. She never forgot the things bad men said or the things they did. She was patient and she waited, vowing revenge. One day, when she was just barely old enough, she went back to the people who treated her so badly. They were asleep and she showed up in their bedrooms with a couple of cans of kerosene."

"Oh, my god!" Marjorie whispered. She wasn't smiling anymore.

"I said shut up," Chuck growled. "I'll handle this!"

Marjorie went quiet, her lips a thin line. I wasn't sure if she was more scared of Chuck or of me. To be certain, I added a kicker. "The trick to doing something like that right," I said, "is you make sure all the exits are nailed shut and doused first."

I didn't get to finish my story. Chuck yanked the wheel and pulled over at a diner. "We can't take you any farther." He popped the lock and my door yawned open.

Before I stepped out, I pushed my luck. "Thank you for the ride. Thanks to you both. You wouldn't happen to have any money you could spare, do you? I haven't eaten since yesterday."

"Get out," Chuck said.

"That girl I mentioned? She was good with remembering lots of things." I looked Marjorie in the eyes. "She remembers names. She remembers the smell of perfume that's so heavy she can taste it. That's the sort of thing that crazy girl with the cans of kerosene would remember."

"You're a liar," Chuck said.

"I never forget a face, Chuck, just like you'll never forget mine, right?"

Chuck ordered me out but Marjorie wasn't so sure I was harmless. I felt a familiar flutter through my stomach and my hands were cold but my death stare was steady. She saw something in my face that made her believe I was capable of something awful, something that might be bad for her. Marjorie was not wrong.

She reached back with her phone and with a shaky hand held it to my bracelet. *Ding!* Forty dollars for me, maybe enough to buy a modest lunch special.

I slipped out of the car. The door would have closed on its own but, trembling and angry, I slammed it as hard as I could.

Grammy once told me, "All stories are real even if they ain't true." The little story I told them wasn't entirely true, but to make it in the world, I had to be ready for anything. The atrocities that occurred in Campbellford had taught me that, and our little town was a tiny slice of the world. Everything was falling apart everywhere.

I didn't want to do terrible things, of course. I wasn't going to be pushed around forever, either. Citizen Security and Safety had my face in their database so whatever they took from me, I would have to accept for the time being. I wasn't prepared to accept every shitty thing fate threw my way, either. Not forever. No one can put up with abuse forever. Eventually, we either run, fight or die.

Clayton Dobbs and what happened in the ditch had taught me harsh lessons about violence. From Mama and Daddy, I learned how to fight. Sissy taught me to be clever. Living with Grammy taught me patience.

I had intimidated a couple of predatory creeps and got forty dollars on the gamble. Still, I doubted I was up to the far greater challenges waiting for me in Atlanta.

CHAPTER FOUR

I passed several cars in the parking lot before checking out the menu in the front window of the diner. Bacon, ham and sausage were scratched through with a bright red marker. What's the point of a diner without the food names that all mean dead pig, shredded, flat, tubed or otherwise?

Sugar was off the menu because of crop failures in the tropics. Someone had scrawled a sun-bleached note that read: *Sugar substitutes are available but don't complain about the price.*

I could see customers inside but the restaurant's front door was locked. A guy sitting in a nearby booth pointed at the door and mouthed something I couldn't understand. I caught on when he pointed at his wrist. The lock had a scanner and it wouldn't pop for me unless I was valid. I didn't have a citizen chip in my bracelet. I wasn't allowed entry unless someone let me in. The customer was still watching me so I waved to him, hoping he would open up for me. He turned back to his meal and pretended I was invisible.

Kismet Beatriz: Not valid.

I gave up on the front entrance before somebody called CSS. Feeling lightheaded and ravenous, I made my way to the rear of the restaurant. There I found two rundown outbuildings. Judging by the wire surrounding it, one used to be a henhouse. The other building looked like an abandoned barn.

I found a big trash receptacle. I was not above dumpster diving but it was locked. Frustrated and hungry, I asked aloud, "Who locks up garbage?"

A woman's voice came out of nowhere, "It's to keep the raccoons out."

Startled, I peered around the dumpster to find a server sitting on the back steps of the building smoking a cigarette. She might have been 35 or 50, one of those people who look haggard and could be younger than they appear if not for the cigarettes. Too much sun and hard living.

She looked me up and down for a few seconds before taking another drag and staring off into space. I knew that look. Anyone who didn't count knew that look.

"You have raccoons?" I ventured.

"Not real raccoons. I think they're all dead by now, at least around here. The locals used to cook 'em up, roadkill stew. Now they hunt 'em."

My gaze went to the big silver padlock, still mystified. The server followed my gaze and let out a thin, wheezing laugh. "By raccoons, I mean you, honey. Scavengers break off from the packs of illegals whenever they come by here. They scrounge for scraps. The boss got fed up so it's locked."

"I'm not an illegal."

"But not a full citizen, am I right? You couldn't get in the front door."

"No shirt, no shoes, no service." I held up my left arm and pulled back the sleeve to expose my bare wrist. "No chip, no privileges."

"As they say, second-class is no class."

"But I've got a little money."

She exhaled a long plume of smoke and stared at me, her eyes red with broken blood vessels. Finally, she sighed. "You like eggs?"

"Real eggs?"

She rolled her eyes at me. "You want a *what* with a *who*? Are you for real?"

I hurried to say, "I like powdered eggs, too."

"Thirty bucks up front. I'll bring you a plate."

"Twenty bucks. Ten now and ten when you deliver."

"Thirty bucks or nothing."

"Thirty bucks, a bottle of water and you let me use the restroom."

"Forty for the bottle of water, too. I can't get you into the toilet. That's customers only." She nodded toward the building I'd taken for a barn. "There's a sink in the garage if you don't make a mess. Don't drink from that tap, though."

"Forty for a meal and a bottle of water? I'm not sure," I said.

"I tell you what, I can nab you some toilet paper as a bonus. I'm sure you can find a comfortable spot out there among the trees."

I was accustomed to relieving myself in the woods. The trick was to find a log to hook your legs over or to hold on to a branch so you didn't pee on your pants. I liked the idea of real toilet paper but I didn't care for the way she told me to go in the woods. When she looked at me, she saw an animal. I glanced at the server's bare wrists. No chip. She wasn't a full citizen, either. She was just like me but with a little bit of power.

I should have left it at that but curiosity got the better of me. "Is your boss one of the Select?"

She chuckled. "You think one of them would eat at a little greasy spoon on the outskirts of Atlanta? I've never met a real boss. I just know Marsha and Benny. Marsha works the breakfast shift with me. Benny's the cook. Some guy comes by to check on the place from time to time but Benny runs the place. Owners? I don't know any owners. That's not how it works."

"How do you think it works?"

"A company that's owned by another company that's owned by a huge corporation runs this diner. A good chunk of the world, too, I suppose. I've never seen one of the Select in here. Real bosses never have a reason to get dirt under their fingernails. They just sit back and watch the money roll in. Sweet gig, huh?"

She took my resentful silence for assent. "Gimme a minute. Gotta finish my coffin nail." She sucked on the cigarette and blew another long plume of smoke. She looked at her cigarette in disgust. "Synthetic.

Just as deadly as ever but not as sweet as the real thing. The ciggies and the food taste bad. Miracle living through better chemistry, my ass. I used to be fat. I miss the reasons to be fat."

She held up her cigarette and stared at it as if it had secrets to reveal. "Sometimes I think the bosses of the world want us all dead and or at least livin' miserable. Misery sucks all the energy away. They only let us have what little we got just so we don't storm their walls. Just as well. I can't make any trouble. My knees are shot."

"You don't want to go all torches and pitchforks on their asses?"

She put a finger to her lips. "Maybe go easy on the T & P talk. You don't know me. For all you know, I could go inside and call the CSS on your skinny ass. Don't be stupid. I need you to live long enough to pay me my forty bucks."

The server sucked down the last of the cigarette and got to her feet. "All the money up front. By the sound of you, I'm not confident you'll last until I get back."

I held out my bracelet and she dug one of her own out of her apron. Before the devices touched, she said, "I'll meet you in the garage at my next break. Wait for me. I can't just put in an order to the kitchen. You'll get the leavings I scrape from customers' plates, you understand?"

I shuddered. Then, I nodded.

"Take your time with the sink and give yourself a good wash. You're sweaty. Benny's car is in there. You touch it, you die. Got it?"

I wanted to smash the server's nose and turn it into a blood fountain. Then I could take her bracelet, force my way into the diner and eat all their greasy food. Instead, I gave her all the money I'd scammed from the creeps. Hunger smashes pride in half. It would be a cold meal swallowed down with bitterness. Still, I was eager to eat something.

My only satisfaction was found in not thanking the server. In the face of indignity and scorn, that compensation was microscopic. I hated to feel helpless but who doesn't?

Secondhand fake powdered eggs and fascism, I thought. *It's what's for dinner.*

CHAPTER FIVE

Inside the garage I changed out of my dusty clothes. The sink was hooked up to a well. I used the pump and a rag to wash up before pulling fresh clothes from my pack. Mama said that in the infantry changing to fresh socks could make the last ten klicks to a long ruck a tad easier. With nothing to do but wait, I washed the shirt I'd worn and twisted it over and over to wring it out.

I didn't taste the water from the pump. I could smell there was something off about it, a strong metallic odor. I decided not to use my filter straw. Better to wait for the water bottle I'd paid for. Giardia and other waterborne diseases were pretty common but in the last several months cholera outbreaks had appeared throughout the South. People blamed the refugees for the spread of disease. The propapundits said without mass immigration, no citizen would get sick.

Grammy taught me otherwise. "Nobody running north had a hand in building the water systems in the detainment centers. They didn't build the waste management in the camps, neither. Everything's been breakin' or broken since I was a girl. It's not a new thing but it's always been a needful thing. Hate is the virus. Seems like pretty near everybody's got *that* fever."

That rang true. One of our neighbors a few farms over was

Clayton Dobbs. As we sat on our porch, Dobbs leaned on our fence and railed on about a refugee who didn't have the energy to keep traveling north. The homeless man hung out at the men's mission in Campbellford.

"I go into town, minding my business, and suddenly I'm getting harassed by this tall-ass man," Dobbs said. "You'd know him if you saw him, wears a battered old suit and a bolo tie. A bolo! Gotta be from Down There! Beggars and takers! They got nothing good to give! I don't know him from Adam but that man has a thumpin' gizzard where his heart should be, botherin' good people just trying to go about their business."

I recognized the phrase 'beggars and takers' from the propapundits. "It's not racism! It's math!" (They always insisted their hatred couldn't be rooted in racism.)

"'Down There,'" Grammy scolded Dobbs, "is code for either genitals or Mexico. Neither is expected to be heard in polite company."

"But the tall man, he's always askin' for money!" Dobbs insisted. "I ain't got no money and neither do you. Nobody does, not enough to spare, anyway. But here's this immigrant embarrassing folks, people who are too poor to paint and too proud to whitewash."

"You ever dared to ask a stranger for money, Mr. Dobbs?" Grammy asked.

"Of course not." Dobbs looked horrified that she would even ask.

"It takes bravery. The beggar is always more embarrassed than the person he's asking, I assure you."

Dobbs ignored my grandmother and ranted on, "Y'all don't understand! These people are dangerous!"

Grammy gave him the side-eye and whispered to me, "Imagine being such a coward you can't bear to hear a person asking you a question. All this fool had to do was say no."

"I've called the CSS twice on that fella," Dobbs whined. "He runs off before they can run him off for good. He was back the next day asking for $5 or $10 from everybody to feed his family!" Dobbs was so worked up, he had to wipe the sweat from his brow and was panting a little when he finished. "Damn immigrants, takin' our jobs, tryin' to live off us — "

"Which is it?" Grammy called back from the porch. "Takin' our jobs or livin' off us?"

Dobbs smiled and wagged his finger. "Mother Beatriz, you are a clever one."

"Not so clever, just not so stupid fearful," Grammy whispered to me again.

"All I'm sayin' is be careful when you venture into town. Beggars used to be just a city thing. Now they're everywhere! That fella is a foreigner up to no good, I guaran-damn-tee!"

Grammy was funny about our neighbor's fears but I understood how Mr. Dobbs felt. I didn't go into town often. When I did, I made sure to walk on the opposite side of the street, walking fast past the Mission. Most beggars were polite but once when I was eleven or twelve a man followed me down the street. With his long gray beard, wild eyes and toothless mouth, the stranger demanded to know who my father was. He followed me for two blocks shouting, "Who's your daddy? Who's your daddy?"

Just the memory of his harassment gave me the shivers.

As it happened, I did go into town a couple of days after Dobbs paid his visit. A tall man in a battered suit wearing a bolo tie stood outside of the Mission. From the other side of the street, it appeared he was asking passersby for help. His voice was inaudible and he did not raise his head to meet anyone's eyes.

On my way back, the tall man was shouting for help as four burly guards attacked him. They shoved him to the ground as he screamed, "You're breakin' my arm! I'm a godly peaceful man of faith and you're doin' this to me? To *me*? I got an arm that's already gibbled and you're breakin' my one good arm!"

The guards dug their batons into his side and shouted at the beggar to cooperate. As far as I could tell, the only order they'd given him was to cooperate. It was hard to figure how he could comply more or harder.

The man cried as they zip-tied his hands behind his back. "It's come to *this*? It's come to this!"

He shouted for help a couple of more times, right up until they pulled a black bag over his head and carried him to a waiting truck. He was quiet after that. I'd heard enough to know that, despite the bolo tie, that man was no immigrant. He had the same soft accent as Clayton Dobbs. If that man had ever even stepped a foot out of Georgia, I'd eat nothing but crow and not complain.

It has come to this, I thought.

I didn't want to dwell on that memory but hunger has a way of gnawing away all other thoughts. Despite my trepidations, the server brought me what I'd paid for. She emerged from the diner just as darkness fell. She stalked in and put my meal on a workbench. True to her word, she dug a bottle of water out of her apron and slammed it down beside the plate of cold powdered scrambled eggs and two stale biscuits.

There were no utensils. "Got a fork for the eggs?"

In the dim light of the garage, her face was just a suggestion among shadows. Still, I could sense her contempt. "I'm tired, my feet hurt and I am not your waitress, girl. I risked my job for you. That's the same as risking my life."

I considered saying a lot of mean things. However, if I got too aggressive, the next hungry girl who tried to buy a cold overpriced meal might not get her cooperation. Though it was true for everyone, the fact that her job and her life were synonymous made me sad. "What's your name?"

"I never told you my name. You don't need to know it. Knowing names only buys people trouble. I'm not interested in aiding, abetting or accomplicing. I got enough trouble."

"I'm Kismet," I said. "My name is Kismet Beatriz. I only wanted to know your name so I could thank you properly."

Her posture changed then. Her shoulders dropped and her head tilted a little to the side. Maybe that was curiosity. Maybe exhaustion. Still, her next words were softer than before. "You don't need to thank me. You paid."

"You could have turned me away or called the CSS. You didn't. Thanks for that, at least."

"Suzanne. I'm Suzanne. You're welcome."

She turned to leave but she paused by the door. "A little advice? Stay off the main roads into the city. The refugees don't know any better so they come up the big highways. There've been so many of them, they would shut a highway down but for the autonomous trucks."

"I don't understand."

"It's different from the way it was. Right and wrong have switched around. Suppose somebody was driving and they hit a non-citizen. In the old days, a crowd could still make trouble for them. CSS found a way around that. Centurions come to the diner sometimes. I heard some laughing about reprogramming the transport trucks. They're just drones. They don't steer around all obstructions. Understand?"

I understood. One of the AUTONAVs had nearly hit me out on the road. "You're saying the trucks will drive into a crowd of refugees."

"It wouldn't be an accident, Kismet," Suzanne told me. "The way the CSS sees it, they're just solving problems by clearing the way. And not a single full citizen will ever have to see the inside of a court. They just call it equipment failure and say, 'Oh, well.'"

Suzanne sighed and shook her head at my naiveté. "Robots don't go to court and citizens don't either, not unless they have a beef with another citizen. It's dangerous out here, kid. I wish you luck but you should give some serious thought to going home and staying there."

"Thank you. I have heard that once already, but I've got somewhere I need to be and it's not at home."

Suzanne bobbed her head and strolled back to the diner. She paused a moment to look up at the darkening sky before returning to work. I imagined that she didn't get many chances to look at the sky. I noticed she limped a little as she crossed the yard. When she couldn't stand all day anymore, what would she do then? Maybe then it would be her scrounging for scraps at the back of a diner. Maybe this same diner, if it didn't go out of business first. After all, how long could a greasy spoon stay open when they couldn't even offer bacon substitutes? I wondered how often Suzanne worried about her future.

Cold eggs are slimy. Cold powdered eggs are worse, like trying to swallow a toad who's not enthusiastic about getting eaten. However, after I broke the biscuits open and scooped the mixture into the bread to make a sandwich, it wasn't as terrible. As Grammy would say, hunger is the best sauce.

The biscuits sat heavily in my stomach. The lightheadedness I'd felt earlier was replaced by nausea. My stomach had become a tight knot and I'd eaten too fast. I didn't want to throw up such an expensive meal so I found a tight spot behind the car and lay down.

I had not intended to fall asleep. When I awoke, a large man stood over me. He did not look happy to see me.

"Hello," I said cheerily as my hand closed on the knife handle to the blade strapped to my forearm.

Suzanne was right. Right and wrong had switched around.

CHAPTER SIX

The big man loomed over me. His hair was pulled back in a ponytail. His bare arms were covered in tattoos, a luxury that made me think he must be quite well off. "What do you think you're doing here, Trouble?"

"I think I fell asleep. Or this is a nightmare. Not sure." I gave him a smile as I got to my feet.

"Been here long?"

"Just passing through."

But he wasn't looking at me. He stared at the empty plate on the floor. "Where'd you get that?"

I shrugged. "I'll just be on my way."

He put a heavy hand on my shoulder. "Hold on. Did Suzanne feed you?"

"I don't know any Suzanne." My grip tightened on the knife. I'd never stabbed anyone but I could picture what would come next. I would twist under his grip to step closer and get his elbow into my armpit, clamp down and drop to one knee as I drove the blade up under his ribs and into his heart.

The big man sighed. "I'm headed into the city. You need a ride?"

"Huh?"

He backed away and gestured for me to grab my pack. "Let's get you away from here."

"I can walk, thanks."

"Better if I drive you. If my boss finds out Suzanne gave away food to a raccoon, that's the end of her job. If the CSS finds out she gave comfort and shelter to a non-citizen, that could be the end of both of us."

"I had a scare recently. I don't want to get in a car with a stranger. My mama told me that."

"Sound advice. I like the color royal blue and I cook food. I used to be an aerospace engineer but then China stopped supplying parts and nobody flies anywhere anymore unless they're pilots chauffeuring the bosses or delivering missiles somewhere at supersonic speed. See? Stranger no more! Whoop-de-do. I just want to go home, kid. I've been cookin' since six and I gotta be back here in the morning at six. Let me drop you off somewhere. That's it."

"So you're Benny."

"Let's just keep our conversation to stuff like me liking royal blue."

"I like the color of clear sky."

"That's azure." He opened the passenger door and left it open as he walked around to the driver's side. "If we're done with the pleasantries, let's get you out of here before I lose the best waitress I ever had."

I climbed in and held my pack in my lap.

"Scoot down so the cams along the highway don't clock you."

I slunk down in my seat as far as I could. Benny yanked my pack up tall to make sure my face was obscured and we took off. The car wasn't as fancy as the sleek low-slung machine Chuck and Marjorie used. Still, it was good to be putting miles behind me, carried along without expending precious energy.

"You got somewhere to go in the city?"

"Nowhere special."

"So where should I drop you?"

"Downtown."

"I can't take you that far. You don't want to go downtown, anyway."

"I don't?"

"There's nothing there but rotting buildings that used to be something. That and the camps."

"There's more than one?"

"You really don't know whether to scratch your watch or check your ass, do you?"

Maybe I should have stabbed you, I thought.

"There's the family camp. That's the smallest, over by the old zoo in Grant Park. The CSS has a camp for female illegals and another for males. Those go all the way from the Downtown Connector over to the Summerhill neighborhood. Then there's a processing center west of the Connector. I don't know who's all in there. Maybe nobody does. The rumor is that there's a prison where people go in but they never come out. I don't know about that. What I do know is, the closer you get to downtown, the more CSS you'll run into. I'll drop you in Midtown, closer to the Circle."

"The Circle?"

"The wall around New Atlanta. It's a safer neighborhood ... sorta. Lots of CSS everywhere so the danger quotient is half up, half down. Used to be a rundown area called Mechanicsville until the Select scooped up all the land and gentrified it. New Atlanta is kinda like a gated community but with castle walls."

As we entered the old city, most of it was dark. I wasn't prepared for my first look at New Atlanta. We drove beside it for a few minutes before I understood what it was. At first, I assumed we were driving around a huge power plant. Brightly lit and patrolled by CSS, the Circle was a huge concrete wall topped by solar panels, wind turbines, water collectors and guard towers. Some sections of the wall were staggered steel bars but most of it was constructed of concrete.

Benny chuckled. "That eyesore is so big, it's pretty much everywhere poor folks aren't."

Everyone knew about the wall. Hearing about it was one thing but seeing it was something else. Still, when he glanced my way with his superior smile, I felt like a rube.

"The wall was the country's last big construction project but the Select don't care much for publicity," he said. "It was banned from the news. Security reasons, they said. Big as it is, the layout is even blurred out on satellite maps."

To my surprise, the wall's gray surface was decorated with sporadic murals. Taggers had hit it with various gang signs and art. I craned my neck to get a better look until Benny told me to sit lower in my seat.

"Most of those paintings happened during construction," he said. "That wall is thirty feet tall. Twenty-seven gates to New Atlanta, but most of them are shut forever, only open in case of fire or something. You can't see it but there's a ton of great houses behind that wall. Most will never see it."

My eyes narrowed with suspicion. He talked like someone who liked to think he knew things no one else knew. "You've been inside?"

"Once. I met a boss in there for something back when I got hired at the diner. They spent billions building that eyesore and wasted another billion to make enough space for a golf course. I made a joke about not being sure whether the walls were to keep the riffraff out or in. Almost lost the job, right then. A sense of humor is not something the Select Few values in their lessers. If you get to meet our betters, don't joke around. They shit themselves blind if they read a sentence without an Oxford comma."

"But you went from flying airplanes — "

"I *designed* aircraft."

"Sorry — "

"Now I'm a short-order cook. I had no training but they figured I'd be a quick learner. I was. I am. You know the most important lesson I learned on the inside of the Circle? They win, we lose, it's over."

"What's over?"

"Everything. Not everybody's got the memo yet but we're finished. Maybe it'll all end in fire or flood. I'm betting everybody finally fades away from malnutrition. Whatever. Years from now, the Select Few will still be putting and puttering around their golf course, laughing about how the losers are all dead and they survived. The bosses may be cockroaches, but cockroaches are survivors. The rest of us are just gettin' by until the final bell rings."

"Do cockroaches have wings?" I asked.

"Huh? I dunno. Why?"

"I need to figure a way to find shelter under their wings."

"They take care of their own. You come near them, they'll smell climber on you. The Select like when people suck up to them but, as a general rule, they *really* hate climbers. The wall's there to keep you out. Remember that." Benny stopped the car just beyond the looming shadow of the big wall and I got out.

"When you've got as much as the Select Few, everybody wants a piece. Cockroaches survive because they've got a hard shell and they stick together. Be careful out there. You never know who you're talking to or who's listening. And one more thing: Never come back to my diner. Never ever."

Benny roared off. The car door handle ripped from my hand and slammed shut as he swept around a corner and disappeared.

Alone in Midtown Atlanta in the middle of the night, I had no place to stay. All I had were Sissy's instructions and the hope that she was okay.

CHAPTER SEVEN

The wall around New Atlanta was impossible to ignore. Navigating the city streets, the concrete barrier was a landmark that indicated which way was north. The searchlights from the guard towers roamed constantly. Its parapets and gates were symbols of power, status and intimidation. The Circle seemed an unassailable castle. Somehow I had to find a way inside.

I walked south, then east. The night was cool and I sensed rain was on the way. I trudged a long time, picking my way through the street names, wary of every stranger I passed. I had a map of Atlanta, a relic from before the wall went up.

There were still green spaces, but they were all occupied by the homeless and watched over by guards. It's funny how much you can tell from a person's posture. By the look of them, the CSS weren't hanging around to protect the homeless. They stood stiffly and glared at them, seeming to dare them to make trouble, eager for an excuse to bust heads.

And I was one of the homeless now, too. According to the propapundits, anyone who disagreed with the new policies — or anyone who wasn't a member of the Select Few — was "part of the problem." Already a target, I hadn't actually done anything rebellious yet.

Judging by the map, I was close to where I was meant to be. It turned out to be the talisman I needed to find a fellow traveler.

"Haven't seen one of those in a long time. Paper? Really?"

I looked up from the map to find a tall woman sitting on a bench by a bus stop.

"Just sayin' you'd be better off payin' for the GPS on your bracelet or gettin' a ride. This city is drowning in streets called Peachtree. You'll never find your way like that."

"No, thanks. I don't have anybody to call."

"That sounds like the beginning or the end of a sad story. Maybe I can give you directions. C'mere and take a load off for a few, will ya?"

I gladly accepted the invitation and sat down heavily.

"Tired?"

"I lucked into a ride but got dropped off farther away than I hoped." I glanced up at the weathered sign over the bus stop. "If I got on the bus, maybe I could get some sleep or at least get a better sense of the city. Daddy always said time spent on recon was seldom wasted. When's the next one due?"

"No bus 'round here."

I sighed. "How about in the morning?"

"No bus then, neither. Atlanta hasn't had public transportation for years."

"Then, can I ask, what are you waiting for?"

"You, darling! Where have you been all my life?"

"Waiting for you, darling," I replied.

We both laughed and I began to relax.

"The street lights still work under the old bus stops so it's a good spot to sit and be seen," she said. "I love to be seen. Nothin' worse in this world than to be invisible, is there?"

"There is not." I smiled. "I see you."

When she returned my smile and I knew I'd come to the right spot.

"Most nights out here mean gettin' a ride from a lonely fella." She laughed and the sound was stronger than it was pretty. "Gettin' a ride and givin' a ride. Sometimes, some waif comes along who looks lost and needs direction."

I didn't know what to say so I said nothing. She extended her hand. "I've forgotten my manners. Chantelle, Chantelle Morrison."

I hesitated and she added, "You okay?"

"Sorry. I feel like I'm a million miles from home and I left my grandmother in the care of a neighbor. She'll be okay for a while but getting here late at night, everything feels like a mistake."

"Like you've started down a rough road and there's no turning back and here you are, talking to a stranger on a bench in the middle of the night?"

"Exactly like that. Sorry."

"Don't be sorry until sorry's necessary."

I told her my name and shook her hand. Her palm was dry and soft and cool, enveloping mine in a gentle grip. Even under the dim glow of the old yellowing lens of the street light, Chantelle was beautiful. Her dress sparkled. Her hair was piled high, a tall hat of ringlets.

She must have seen my expression change as the realization hit.

"Look at you, all wide-eyed. Y'all never met a trans-person before?"

I shrugged. "One. My Uncle Casey."

"That right?"

"After the Mason-Dixon Decree, he moved. He could have stopped in Maine or New York but he said he was fed up and just kept on going all the way to Canada."

"Out of one war and into another, huh?"

The Water War wasn't much of a war. Ordered to stand down, the Canadian Armed Forces offered little resistance to American advances. "Like an eager girl on prom night," Grammy said.

Scattered groups of Canuck rebels had lost themselves to the wilderness so there were occasional attacks on rail lines and convoys. I had a hard time imagining my tiny Uncle Casey roughing it in the woods to count himself among the defenders of his new home.

"Y'all got a question? Go ahead. If a handsome man or woman comes by, I might have to conclude our business quick, but it's a slow night." She gave me a wink.

I wasn't certain if she was serious. "After the Mason-Dixon Decree, how are you still here?"

"You mean how come your poor uncle had to run away but here I am, big and bold and out in front of God and everybody, going about the devil's business?"

"Well, yeah."

"The Mason-Dixon decision was an awful thing. That broke up my community. A bunch of my friends had to pick up and run north, runnin' for their lives even though they never bothered anybody. Love is love and marriage is an affirmation of love. I learned that in church long before a bunch of bigots decided to make religion all about being mean. Used to be we were all sinners and no one was supposed to cast stones."

"My grandmother says you can understand a person's religion easily. How much time do they spend kicking somebody when they're down instead of helping them up?"

"My old pastor would say the kickers are the kind of believers who smile on Sunday but shoot you on Monday. Some people enjoy a snootful of adultery and divorce but start yellin' when you admit you are how God made you. I am how God made me and my God does not make trash. "

"So the CSS really don't bother you?"

"They bother me plenty but they don't arrest me. Centurions can exercise discretion in Mason-Dixon matters. Sometimes I gotta pay with a little money and once in a long while, damn their leering eyes, I have to give 'em some sugar to shut 'em up. But I pass. If you pass for what you were born to be, they pretty much leave you alone."

"Doesn't sound fair to Casey."

"It's not fair, but it's not about what we want. It's what the citizens want."

"Citizens lobbied hard for the Mason-Dixon decision. The Select voted overwhelmingly."

"Yeah, they really taught us something, didn't they?"

"What's that?"

"Making progress is like pushing a car uphill. You gotta keep pushing or it'll roll back, right over you."

Chantelle smiled and patted my arm with what seemed like genuine affection. "When the people in charge make those decisions, they're in a room that's all polished oak. Their desks are mahogany. They're in a room with a lot of brittle old men and dusty women. When they write those laws, that's when they're being who they think they should be. People do a lot of silly things when they think they're living up to a made-up ideal. But out here, down in the dirt? Different story. Down here, people are who they really are."

"Different how?"

"The nights are lonely and I am a *beautiful* Jezebel. When they say Jezebel in church, the tone is mean. When they're out at night driving around in their fancy cars and the seat next to them is cold?" She laughed. "That's when things get real. The centurions leave me alone because the citizens who stop to give me a ride want me out here. They condemn us in the day. Sunlight makes 'em forget. When the moon comes up, they remember how sad they'd be without me."

"Doesn't it make you mad?"

"Mostly, I feel bad for them. They're denying their true nature. I get it, used to do that myself. I used to be an angry man named Roger. Used to work for the Circle. Used to start and end my day with the pledge to keep the Circle unbroken. Hard to believe now, huh?" She tossed her hair, smiled and batted her eyelashes coquettishly.

"The Select Few drove a lot of good people into Old Atlanta and underground. That's gonna change."

"When?"

"If all goes startlingly well, I think it will happen. Be like a were-wolf, Kismet. Look to the full moon. Things'll change, they always do. Every dog has his day and every drag queen gets their applause. Not gonna lie, though. The Lord tells me to be patient and wait for Her Grace. The long wait can feel like gettin' served hot shit on a cold plate!"

I never heard God referred to as female. When I told Chantelle so, she giggled. "Of course, God is a woman! Gotta be. You know how I know? She's so patient with Man."

"You ever work inside the Circle's wall, Chantelle?"

She bobbed her head.

"Ever talk to a citizen like this?" I asked. "To one of the Select, I mean?"

"They aren't great listeners," she replied.

"Just once, it would feel kind of great to tell one of them I felt sorry for them — "

"Oh, no, honey! Citizens only want to hear 'yes, sir,' and 'how high up the alimentary, ma'am?'"

I burst out laughing and Chantelle joined me. After a moment, she gave me a long sober look and added, "Seriously, though, never tell a citizen you're sad for them. That's the worst thing for them to hear. They can't handle that. Got the worst beating of my life the night I made that mistake. They don't want your pity no matter how gentle you say the words and how kindly you may mean it."

"Thanks for the advice."

"You feeling more comfortable?"

I stiffened but lied and told her I was okay.

"The parks are either detention camps or heavily patrolled. You want to keep heading east on this road some more. If you get to Ponce, you've gone too far."

"Ponce?"

"Ponce de Leon Avenue. Home Depot, Trader Joe's and Whole Foods all moved inside the Circle. Look for those signs. You'll find a place to lay your head at the old Home Depot."

"Really? Why there?"

"Those abandoned buildings are official shelters now. The old food stores don't take newcomers past dusk but you'll find a space in the old Home Depot. That's your next step. Trust me."

"But I have to get into the Circle — "

"Getting in and out isn't easy, Kismet. An opportunity will present itself."

"Thank you, Chantelle."

"When you lie down, wind the straps of your pack around your arm or something. Use it for a pillow and you won't lose it. And don't take those hiking boots off. Somebody might try to gank those from you."

I wore my mother's boots, the same she'd worn when she came back from her first tour of duty in Mexico. I felt sorry for people who didn't like their parents. Without them, I felt like a bird who couldn't fly.

"You still okay, Kismet? Your eyes are lookin' a little bit wet. There's a storm comin' but it's not raining yet."

I said nothing. Instead, I hugged her.

Chantelle patted me on the back gently. "It's tough out here. Y'all going to have to be tougher. The Select ask too much of us and give too little kindness in return. See what God puts in your path and what you can do with it. Maybe She's got big plans for you, too."

I pulled back and wiped the tears from my eyes.

"I know how deep and raw the deal is," Chantelle said. "I came to Atlanta from Lilburn, Georgia. Got here in the back of a truck." She got a faraway look in her eyes, as if she could look through the dark, clear to a brighter future. "The Select keep pushin' us down, but people are like springs. All this time they're keepin' us down is just building up more energy and heat. All this friction they give us is gonna backfire."

"Revolution?"

"A reckoning. Rumors of torches and pitchforks are already on the wind. The meaner the Select get, the harder and faster the reckoning will come."

In the distance, thunder rolled and rumbled.

Chantelle gently brushed a strand of hair from my eyes. "Their time's runnin' out." She reached up to her own pile of ringlets, withdrew a small black clip and slipped it into my hair. "There. That will help you see clearly."

A little yellow coupe slid up to the bus stop. Chantelle frowned and sighed. "It's showtime."

The passenger side window rolled down. A woman with a short shock of peroxide blonde hair called out, "Hey! Chantelle! Need a ride?"

Chantelle squeezed me tight once more and stood. I hadn't realized how tall she was. She towered over me. "Good luck, Kismet! Stay safe and be patient. Full moon's comin'! DHD, baby!"

I'd heard of DHD several times from travelers who'd begged for water at my grandmother's gate. Refugees were our most reliable source of news. The catchphrase came up a lot. When people felt safe, they even used it as an expression of greetings and farewell among friends.

Don't hope. Do.

CHAPTER EIGHT

I found the old Home Depot in time to beat the rain. A CSS officer manned the gate. The glow from his pad made him look ghostly. He ordered me to turn to the door, to stand still and to refrain from smiling. I wasn't in the mood to smile, anyway.

A quick flash from above the door made me blink. Biometric scan.

The result popped up on the guard's screen immediately. "Kismet *Beatriz*, huh?"

"Yes, sir."

"Says here your parents are citizens."

"Military status, yes. My mother, father and big sister have all served, yes."

"Why didn't you join up?"

I wasn't in the mood to discuss my family history with a stranger. "As far as I know, it's still a choice, sir."

He smirked. "They're talking about bringing back the draft so maybe you won't have that choice much longer."

"Does that mean everyone would become a citizen?"

"That's probably the question that's holding it up. Says here you were born in Old Mexico."

This wasn't idle curiosity. He was trying to rattle me, to shake loose a mistake. "When I was born, the state was still called New Mexico."

"We should never have made that concession. Do you agree?"

The guard's question could have been a trap. It wasn't relevant to whether I should gain admittance to the shelter. I risked not answering his question and stuck to what he needed to know. "My parents are both Army. I was born at White Sands. Can I go in? It's going to rain and — "

"White Sands ... legal and on base?"

"Yes, sir."

He asked my date of birth. That information had to be on his screen but I told him, anyway. After a pause, I asked if there was a problem.

"No problem," he said. "I'm deciding whether to believe you. Records can be faked. You're arriving in the middle of the night. Lotsa refugees would kill to get into a shelter, especially with another storm coming in."

I shrugged. "I'm from Campbellford, just north of here."

"Most refugees are headed in the direction you came from."

"I'm not a refugee." At least, I wasn't the kind of refugee he was supposed to worry about.

"A word of advice: With a last name like Beatriz, expect to get stopped and questioned. We're getting pretty sick of people who look like you."

"What can I do about that?"

"If I were you, I'd head north and I wouldn't look back."

"That's not what my family fights for," I replied.

"Another word of advice," he said sternly, "Watch your tone when you're talking to a CSS agent. Now go."

I couldn't have been more civil. What more could he want from me? It seemed he was waiting for me to thank him. I remained silent. Finally, he sighed and waved me on. The lock buzzed and the door to the shelter opened just as the wind picked up and a torrent began to fall.

He called after me, "Welcome to the Hobo Hilton!"

The lights were dim but still bright enough to pick my way through all the bodies on the floor. If not for the snoring, coughing and rustling, this refuge from the rain would look more like a morgue, or maybe the scene of a bomb blast.

All the spots along the walls were taken by people who preferred to sit while they slept. I found a spot that was more sparse, surely because it was directly under a spotlight. The concrete was cool but the air was too warm from all the people crammed into the shelter, warming the stale air with each breath.

Remembering Chantelle's advice, I took off my boots just long enough to massage my aching feet, then hurriedly laced them up again. I considered digging into my pack to fashion a makeshift mattress out of my clothes.

Out of the darkness, someone shushed me. From another direction, someone scolded, "Stop your fussin'!"

I didn't think I could sleep but I went still. Eventually, I fell into a fitful sleep full of anxious dreams. In one vision, I was rushing to get somewhere. I was late for something but I didn't know what. When I looked behind me, someone was following, gaining ground, closing on me.

I woke up for a moment. My left shoulder ached from sleeping on the hard floor so I turned on my right shoulder and somehow collapsed into asleep again.

My father taught me how to control my dreams, a feat I had not fully mastered. "The key to becoming a lucid dreamer," Daddy told me, "is to ask throughout the day, is this real? Is this happening? When you ask that question so much that it seeps into your dreams, you've got the key to waking within the dream and gaining control of it."

Sometimes I slipped into that lucid state of consciousness. When I did, for a short time before waking, I could fly. When I told my father of this accomplishment, he hugged me close. "When your body is resting but your mind breaks the bonds of gravity and dream logic, flying is the best feeling you can have, isn't it?"

"It was great," I said. "When it happened I felt so..." I struggled to describe it.

"Free," he said. "When you fly, you're free."

"Exactly!"

"The world is screwed so tight, it might collapse in on itself," Daddy told me. "Keep lucid dreaming in your toolkit. It can help with lots of things."

"How?"

"It's good to have a place to retreat to. No matter what goes down, you can bring yourself up. It's eased my mind, gave me time to work on problems, even got me through boot camp and cooled down a whole lot of hot trouble since."

But that night in the shelter, freedom and flight were denied me. Worry took control of my ship of dreams and would not relinquish the helm.

In the last reverie, in the nightmare I would remember best, Grammy stood alone in a field bare of crops. I couldn't go to her for some reason. I yelled for her to come to me. Instead, she wandered away. I wasn't sure if she was looking for me, confused or ignoring my cries. I think I was invisible to her, maybe a ghost. I begged her to come back. Squinting against bright light, it seemed Grammy was swallowed by the sun.

We come from starlight and ultimately we will be returned to the stars as stardust. I read that somewhere, I don't remember where. When I awoke, I worried I'd somehow caught a signal that Grammy was dead.

I never had bad dreams about Mama and Daddy when they went away. They were called to duty more often than they were home so their absence was normal. However, when Sissy left to join the Air Force, I began to have nightmares about her. I was sure my sister would be killed in a plane crash or get blown up by some unseen enemy. My sleeping brain came up with gory scenarios. Sometimes, I woke up screaming.

Grammy would come into my room and place a cool hand on my sweaty forehead to soothe me. I would babble about what I'd seen and my grandmother would always say the same thing, "Dreams are just dreams. Sleep now. *Sleep*."

When I woke from the vision of my grandmother getting swallowed by a star, I wasn't so sure that dreams were mere figments.

The spotlight above me had powered up to deliver a dazzling light that made me wince. No wonder the place I'd made my bed had been available. In the distance, someone was banging on something and yelling. Around me, everyone stirred, yawning, stretching and scratching.

The banging got closer. Above the noise, a man yelled, "7 a.m.! On your feet! Rise and grind, feed and fuel. Out by 8, pay your dues, back by noon!"

The crowd parted to make way for a man hammering the inside of a steel trash can with a baton. It was the CSS officer who'd been on the gate when I walked in around 3 a.m. I'd got almost four hours. It felt like I'd slept four minutes.

"Make your way to the exits, grab your grub and grab a vest. Out at 8! Back by noon!"

A man and a woman to my right appeared to be together, already gathering their things. They both had sleeping bags and were in the process of rolling them up. An air about them made me think the couple knew the routine. I caught the woman's eye and asked why we had to be back by noon.

"First night?"

"First night in Atlanta, yeah."

"It's not all like this. It is a lovely city," she said.

"Used to be, anyway," her partner grumbled. "You can pay for breakfast. That way you don't have to come back by noon. I don't recommend it. Better to put in the four hours of work. The food is bad and there's not enough of it. Worse, it's way overpriced."

"What if I skip breakfast?"

"You stay the night, it's part of the package so you pay, either way. May as well take the lousy food." She smiled brightly. "It's the way it is."

"That's Miranda," the man said. "I'm Mike. My wife is a philosopher. Good thing she has a happy disposition."

"Might as well laugh as cry," Miranda said.

Mike made a face. "Balances me out."

"We have a deal," the woman added. "Only one of us can panic at a time. If we both lose it, we may as well walk into the sea."

The man looked at her fondly. "She's pulled me back from killing myself a couple of times now."

It seemed a strange admission. Back in Campbellford, no one would admit to suicidal thoughts unless they wanted the rumor spread all over town. People who live in small places have little to entertain themselves. We either turn to each other or we turn on each other. I had assumed it would be different in the big city, that strangers would be more wary of each other. The Slow Apocalypse was not an urban or a rural phenomenon, though. It changed all of us.

"C'mon, people! Soup's on and it's getting cold!" The CSS man called.

I'd been wiping the sleep from my eyes on his first pass. This time I paid the guard more attention. He wore a big hat that was not part of the regulation uniform.

After he passed by, I whispered, "Is that guy really CSS?"

"Sure is," Mike replied.

"I've never seen one with a hat like that," I said.

"He's old," Miranda explained, "Old and old school. It's a state trooper's hat. I guess he used to be one of them before all the police became CSS. Even nasty bastards can hold on to a bit of nostalgia."

"Careful, Miss Sunshine," Mike chided her gently. "Nasty words could ruin your reputation for seeing the best."

"Pardon my husband. Sometimes he confuses my sunny disposition with stupidity." She gave him a hard look. "I choose to smile despite the stupidity of others."

Her smile faded quickly as the guard stood over a still figure not far away. "If you're not gettin' up, you better be dead!"

The man on the floor *was* dead.

I stood and stared, unsure of what should be done. The dead man's lips were blue, his face ghostly white. By the twisted look on his face, I was sure he had died in terrible pain.

The guard did not remove his state trooper's hat. Instead, he cursed, long, loud and imaginatively. He said terrible things about the dead man's mother. Other than venting, the display seemed pointless. I said so to Mike and Miranda.

"It's not pointless," Miranda told me. "Look at it from Old Hat's point of view. They all do it. It makes their lives easier."

Mike rolled his eyes. "Yeah ... or he's just a dick. We better get going unless you want to get pulled into digging a grave for that guy. I'd rather not. He was the one coughing hard last night. That guy needed medical. He was yelling for help. Didn't get it."

Miranda bent to finish filling her backpack. Everyone hurried to get away from the dead man. No one but me seemed to spare the corpse a glance.

As we walked toward the exit, Miranda caught my horrified look. She patted me on the shoulder and whispered, "It's the way it is."

"I don't know how you smile in the face of such ... casualness."

"You can fight the tide or tread water and learn to accept forces greater than yourself. Accepting the way things are makes me peaceful."

I didn't feel peaceful. I wanted to fight the tide.

CHAPTER NINE

Once we were outside the building, I stuck with Mike and Miranda. They knew what to expect and seemed to be the only friendly faces in sight. We got in line for breakfast and the line was long. Every man wore a beard, usually quite ragged. Some younger children cried. I noticed the older children looked thin. When I remarked how well-behaved the little ones appeared, Mike observed that they were probably too scared or too tired to cry.

"The Select won't need so many of Citizen Security forces in another generation," he whispered. "Once they teach all the kids that they're helpless and their only choice is to surrender, the elite will have nothing to worry about, not from us."

Miranda swatted his shoulder and gave her husband a stern look that silenced him. Then she turned her hard glare on me. "If you repeat that, we'll deny it."

Surprised by her sudden change in mood, I tried to assure them I wasn't there to make trouble.

Mike bobbed his head and stared at his feet. "I spoke too loud, too soon, too much. Sorry, Miranda."

Miranda studied me as if she could peer into my bones. "People disappear all the time, you know. Rumor is the people who go away leave this world in much worse ways than on a concrete floor in the night."

I thought again of the beggar outside the Mission back in Campbellford and how quiet he became after the black bag was yanked down over his face. "People are disappearing?"

"*Sh!* Just wait for breakfast and if you must speak, speak of pleasant things."

"Like what?"

"Like the fact that you're getting fed. We should all be grateful for what we have."

After another moment, Miranda seemed to reconsider her words. "Sorry if I came across too harsh. We only just met you. Mike lets his mouth get ahead of his brain sometimes. Making a little fun of Old Hat in whispers is one thing but sedition is another."

Her big grin returned as quickly as it had disappeared. I didn't trust it anymore, though. What I'd first taken as sunny optimism and endurance, I now saw as collaboration. That smile, as empty as a slogan, was born not of bravery but from fear.

The Select had replaced the Elect. It was said the elite had tired of our whining about all the things we did not have. Someone like Miranda would probably survive, smiling to the end of the world, a cheery worker drone come what may. She'd never be honest. She'd never admit that while it's good to appreciate what you have, it isn't right for the oppressors to demand we settle for next to nothing. Forced gratitude is every bit as satisfying as a forced apology.

Miranda stood ahead of me in line. Her smile got even wider as she handed me a bowl. "Don't forget to count your blessings."

I was familiar with the term soup kitchen. I did not expect soup for breakfast. It was a thin broth, lukewarm, with a sparse infusion of carrots, potatoes and split pea flavoring. There was nothing to drink except for the soup and there were no spoons. I tipped the bowl back and drank.

There were two paths beyond the soup line. One was toward a cashier. That line was short. The longer line was for us to pay with our labor.

"One night's sleep and a meal paid for with half a day's work sounds fair, doesn't it?" Miranda burbled.

Several people within earshot hissed their disapproval but no more words were exchanged. Though the day had only begun, everyone seemed exhausted and ill-tempered.

I excused myself to join a line to a portable toilet. When I finally got inside, the little cube smelled of feces and a chemical spray I assumed was designed to cleanse the toilet seat. If it was supposed to negate the fumes emanating from human waste, it failed miserably.

There was no water to wash my hands but I put my hands beneath a device on the wall that issued a dollop of hand sanitizer and a blue light meant to kill germs. I'd been quick but the next person pounded on the door before I could exit the cube.

I joined a new line, careful to avoid the one Mike and Miranda had taken. In a moment, two homeless people strode down the line, one handing out vests, the other giving out sticks with spikes on the end.

A skinny guy wearing a wide-brimmed straw hat fell in behind me. "Clean-up duty for us today."

"What do we do?"

"Pick up litter with the sharp stick. The CSS used to walk down the line to hand out the sticks. Then one day there was a riot. Two were killed and one guard lost an eye. After that, the homeless hand out the sticks to the homeless."

I turned to look at the man. He wasn't much older than me. Someone had broken his nose and it had not set quite right. His eyes were a brilliant blue but it was distracting how his nose appeared to be pointing off to the left. The man might have been handsome in an interesting way but for his smile. When he grinned at me, his teeth were the color of mud.

"I've never seen you before," he said.

"I've never been here before."

"That would explain it." He offered his hand and I shook it. "Name's Jason. People call me Picasso, cuz of the nose."

"Kismet. Which do you prefer? Jason or Picasso?"

"Jason, if you call me Picasso in a mean way. Picasso, if it's a friendly nickname. You know Picasso?"

"I can call you Picasso and make it sound friendly. Never knew anybody with a name like that."

"You get the reference?"

"Sure. I've seen pictures of the pictures."

"Refreshing. Most people don't know the paintings."

"Where I come from, there's nothing to do but read. My grandmother insisted I learn so I did."

"Nothing to do but read?" he echoed. "You sound like somebody from New Atlanta."

I shook my head. "Nope. I'm from Campbellford, up north a little."

"Never heard of it."

"That's why there's nothing to do but read."

"Sounds like heaven. Why'd you leave?"

"Because there was nothing to do but read. What are the vests for?"

"We don't get citizen chips but the vests do. Once you clip on the vest, you're tracked. First, you get on the back of a truck. They'll take you where they want you to be. You pick up garbage and put it in the bag they give you. Around noon, the truck's horn will blare. That's your cue to head back. The clip on the vest will unlock. Then you put the vest, your stick and the bag of garbage on the back of the truck. Then you're done for the day."

"Labor so cheap, it's slave labor, huh?"

Picasso smirked. "That's some high-toned and sassy T&P talk. I like that in a girl."

"T&P?"

"Torches and pitchforks," he said. "You don't hear enough of that around here.

"We spoke more freely where I'm from."

"The villagers whisper about torches and pitchforks when they dream of going after the monsters in the high castle. I dream of guillotines."

"What do you do when you're not dreaming, I mean, for the rest of the day?"

"Catch as catch can," Picasso shrugged.

"What does that mean?"

"Officially? I look for work. Unofficially, that well is dry so I beg. Not much luck unless it's a citizen out and about. Sometimes they come out, slumming for the thrill of poverty tourism."

"I don't know why that would be fun for them."

"Are you kidding? It must be a thrill to see the end of the world and not get any on you. Some Select come out of the castle for some fresh air. They might throw a bone or a crumb. Just be careful not to ask a military citizen for spare change. They don't have much more than us and some are pretty mad about it. Ask them by mistake and you could get a broken nose." Picasso touched his nose and winked.

"Most days the truck drops us off so far afield I have to spend the better part of the afternoon making my way back here to sleep. Then the world spins around again and, if I'm lucky, I'm back in this line talking to a pretty girl and givin' her the what's what."

The way he leered at me, I wondered if it was really a military citizen who gave him the reason for his nickname.

"I'm not interested in getting your what," I said.

"Kismet, there are two kinds of people: Those who understand that life is short so you may as well grab what fun you can and those who lie down and die. Me? I'd like to lie down and not die." He leaned closer and whispered, "They say don't hope, do, but the Slow Apocalypse makes me horny. I say, don't hope. Do me."

"Gross!" I stepped back, grimacing. Picasso's breath smelled of rot. "That's not what DHD is about!"

He shrugged. "So you'd rather die than slip away someplace with me after dark?"

"Correct."

"Harsh. Things keep going the way they go, I could be the last man on Earth someday soon. If you end up as the last woman, I'll ask again."

I glared at my new acquaintance. "I've heard transgressives get sent to the re-education camps in Kentucky."

Picasso smirked. "Church Camp, they call it. You clear brush or work the synthetic food farms. Doesn't sound too bad to me. Three hots and cot and, apparently, sometimes they have orgies in the woods."

"*What?*"

"Hey, you put all the freakified people together, something juicy's gonna happen."

"Gross times ten. Plus, I doubt that's true. If you get an STD, the CSS declares you a bioweapon and exiles you south of the border."

Picasso shrugged. "Oh, well. When nothing ventured, nothing fails miserably. Friends, then?"

"Friends, sure." I smiled but my smile was only as genuine as Miranda's grin. Was Picasso a bad guy? I couldn't say with certainty but I didn't think he was a particularly good one. He was so eager to ingratiate himself, I distrusted his motives. It was possible he was just another person trying to survive, looking for sex, comfort and companionship in troubled times.

It was equally possible Picasso was a spy for CSS, trying to entrap me. Security and safety were not for people like me.

Sissy had warned me to trust no one. "A friend today can be a traitor tomorrow. Trust me. I'll make a path for you."

It was a lonely path.

CHAPTER TEN

A dozen people crammed themselves into the back of the truck I boarded. We were packed in so tightly, someone sat on my left foot. There was barely anywhere to move so I didn't make a fuss. Soon, my foot fell asleep. I wished I could sleep right along with it, numb to the world.

Only one guard drove us to our assignments. Most of the people on the truck looked quite young or very old. Half-starved and already exhausted at the beginning of the day, few looked like they were up to mounting much resistance to the Select. Through our vests, we were all chipped and we couldn't take them off until we'd earned our keep.

One man toward the front began to mutter angrily under his breath. Then he got louder, descending into a rant about how bad the food had been. "Thin soup and a bit of stale synth bread and they think they own us! I guess they do if we let 'em. Look at us, shoved in here like cattle to the slaughter. These vests may as well be collars ... or brands!"

The man's beard was matted and his lips were wet with drool. I wondered if he'd somehow gotten hold of moonshine or suffered a mental illness. His sentiments were not a revelation so why risk saying out loud what was supposed to be a whisper at most?

An old man near me muttered something about how right he was. "Collars, leashes ... or tattooed numbers on our arms."

A woman warned the old man not to encourage the complainer. Other voices rose to shush them all.

It was too late. The drooling man had all the encouragement he needed. He ranted on, repeating his complaints about the food at the shelter.

An older woman struggled to her feet, balancing against the rocking of the truck over potholed streets. "Shut up! You're a trouble-maker, blaming all your troubles on somebody else!"

The man smiled and waved a finger at the scold. "See that? Do you all see that? In every crowd, there's always one or two brave enough to stand up and defend the Select, as if they need your help to shove us down and keep us down."

"Shut up, I said!" The old woman scowled and cursed.

He gave a bitter, guttural laugh. "Every time. There will always be collaborators hoping for mercy. They never get any slack, though. As if they'd ever let you inside the castle gates! You'll always be on the wrong side of history and that damn wall!"

The truck stopped abruptly and a few people, looking relieved to escape, stepped down from the truck.

The drooling man waved at them." Go perform your community service for the sin of being poor!"

The truck idled for a few minutes, unmoving.

Picasso looked at me and whispered, "Trouble's brewing. Keep your head down."

It was getting warm. We all shifted uncomfortably. The woman sitting on my foot shifted her weight and I got my foot out from under her.

Someone banged on the back of the truck and two CSS officers appeared.

"Here we go," Picasso whispered. "Don't look them in the eyes. They're like wolves. They'll take it as a challenge."

I hung my head. Neither of the guards was willing to get into the back of the crowded truck. I don't think they were afraid. It was prob-ably the smell that repelled them.

A CSS officer climbed up to get a better look at us. The centurion pointed at the man who had ranted so vehemently. "Hey! Seditionist! We've got you recorded. C'mon out. We need to talk."

The man shook his head and lowered his gaze. "I didn't say nothing important. Just letting off steam."

The older of the two CSS officers stepped up on the truck's tailgate and offered a kind smile. "It's no big deal. C'mon, now. You don't want to hold up all these nice people. If they don't start working cleanup soon, we'll have to keep them longer until they put the hours in. Nobody wants that bother."

Several men near their target grumbled and the old woman who had scolded him stood again. "I can bear witness to confirm what he said! He said awful things."

The drooling man seemed to talk to himself for a moment. "No badge numbers. CSS has no badge numbers, no names. That's how you know ... they do what they want. The law used to mean something. It was supposed to be for everybody."

The officer smiled. "I've got a name. My name is Martial. Martial Law. Don't make me come in there and get you."

"Anything they want. The biggest crime is to disrespect even one of them."

"C'mon, buddy! Don't make me say please."

"What is there to talk about?"

When I glanced up, the CSS man was surveying all of us with a sour look on his face. I wondered if he would wade into the back of the truck and swing his baton indiscriminately.

"Cooperate or you'll be charged with impeding my investigation. I have to make sure you're not on the side of the folks who assassinated our president. Anyone who helps you will be arrested."

This is how they want us to feel all the time, I thought. *As long as we feel powerless and paralyzed, they'll stay in control.*

Those around the drooling man had had enough. Two men on either side grabbed an arm. Another rose behind him to slip an arm around his throat to yank him to his feet. He resisted briefly until Picasso leaned forward and, with a vicious slap, tagged the drooling man in the groin. The seditionist grunted in pain and almost lost his footing. A woman prodded him forward with the blunt end of her stick.

The man drooled some more as he was pushed toward the tailgate. "There you go. Just a chat. That's all we need. That wasn't so hard, was it?"

He fell into the waiting arms of the CSS. The centurion smiled as he threw the man off the back of the truck. I heard a wet smacking sound that made me shiver. I don't know how I knew, but I was sure that was the sound of a human skull bouncing off concrete.

The truck got into gear and pulled away. I looked back to get a glimpse. Three guards surrounded the man. Their victim appeared unconscious. He certainly was not resisting. It was not an interrogation. It wasn't an arrest, either. They beat him.

Citizen Security and Safety's bloodlust was well-known. I'd watched a report on a protest in Seattle with my grandmother once. As the CSS brutally attacked and maced peaceful protesters, Grammy's mouth became a thin line. "I hope your parents are fighting forest fires right now. I'd hate to think they're in the middle of all that."

"You think Mama and Daddy are in danger?"

Grammy almost laughed and pointed a crooked finger at the screen. "Naw, they're plenty safe. Look at those protesters takin' their medicine. God! The propapundits don't call it assault or torture or attempted murder. They call what happens to them getting 'roughed up.' Does *that* look like anyone's pulling their punches or even trying to arrest anybody?"

And so it was with the man in my truck who had dared to complain. Did the CSS serve themselves alone or was that day's beating a demonstration meant for the rest of us? Probably both.

It made me sad to think it was even possible that a man could be assaulted so savagely to educate me, to silence me. My melancholy soon turned to anger when I caught a look from the old woman who had spoken against him. She'd volunteered to act as a witness but the CSS had no need of witnesses or trials.

The propapundits would never report the beating death of one seditionist. News like that only reached us in Campbellford thirdhand from refugees who personally witnessed such savagery.

The Select benefited from a divided nation but their methods were too brutal. They were so weak, they couldn't even let one powerless homeless man's words stand. Perhaps the Select's inhumanity held the seed of their demise.

Bumping through Atlanta's potholed streets, I brooded. What could one person do in the face of so many problems? Since the assassination of their president, protests against the Select were deemed unlawful. Peaceful demonstrations always ended in blood. Mass arrests were made. People disappeared and faceless rebel groups were blamed for the dead. Raised voices were quickly silenced.

When they pushed that man into the arms of the CSS, I had looked away. Though others had ushered him to the guards, my silence counted me among the collaborators. Complicity, the seed of my shame, blossomed into rage.

I looked again to the old woman who had been so eager to condemn the man. Her self-satisfied grin made me want to avenge a stranger. I had my parent's knives. I wanted to cut that smug look off her face.

But I had other places to be.

CHAPTER ELEVEN

A fter bumping through Atlanta's streets for another few minutes, I jumped down from the truck to stand in the shadow of the Circle's wall. To my right was a checkpoint beneath an opening in the wall: Gate 27.

A single CSS officer stood in her guard shack, not sparing me a glance. Several large signs warned that security was high. *Have identification ready: Roll up your sleeve* and *Intruders will be shot* figured prominently.

To my left, the street opposite Gate 27 was closed to traffic. Several signs warned of roadwork and construction but no one was in sight. It seemed a stark juxtaposition: the Circle was complete but Atlanta's infrastructure was in shambles.

Picasso climbed off the back of the truck, stepping down carefully. He seemed pained. I hadn't noticed his limp while we stood in line. I asked him if he was hurt.

"Sitting for too long makes me achy."

I thought of Grammy, how she grunted when she got up or sat down and was similarly stiff until she got moving. However, I guessed Picasso couldn't be more than 22 or 23 years old.

"I was here for the riots," he explained. "Got caught in the crush and got in some scraps. Never got it fixed right. Rolled my ankle bad last year and never got over it. Met a guy on the street once who used to be a doctor in Guatemala. He told me that with new cells replacing old cells, we're new people every seven years. I guess if I just wait, it'll be fine."

He leaned on his spiked stick as he grabbed several garbage bags from the truck. It soon pulled away and, before he could hand me a bag, my vest buzzed.

Picasso grinned. "Feel that? It means you're on the clock and not moving. Don't let it buzz too long or you'll be out here in the heat for hours more than you need to be. Sometimes they send out a CSS guy just to yell at you for practice."

"Sounds pleasant."

He pointed to litter that had collected at the base of the wall. "They like it pristine around the gates. Looks like lots of litter from the hordes blew in last night."

"Hordes? You mean the great migration of people fleeing the tropics?"

Picasso shrugged. "Hordes, migration, parade ... whatever you want to call it."

"People. I prefer to call them people."

"You got a bleeding heart?"

"I've seen some things. Haven't you?"

Not waiting for an answer, I turned my back on Picasso and began collecting garbage. The detritus consisted of food ration wrappers, dead leaves, pieces of paper, scatterings of red ribbons and a few empty water bottles. Angry, I stabbed everything and slipped them into the garbage bag.

As I stepped closer to the wall, the CSS officer came out of her shack and took a picture of me. She peered at her phone for a moment, shielding the sun with her hand so she could read the scan. I wondered if I was in trouble for getting too close. The wall was a sheer face. New Atlanta's security was in no danger from me. The guard disappeared into her shack. Relieved, I realized then that I'd been holding my breath.

Behind me, Picasso cursed. I turned to see two CSS vehicles park at the top of the closed street. One was a big box truck. The driver, a small man carrying a large rifle, opened the rear door. Men and women wearing jumpsuits of several colors piled out.

"Work gang," Picasso called. "Stay away from them. They can compromise you just by asking for something. If you don't spit on them right away, the CSS may want to talk to you."

I nodded and went about my business. However, I was too curious not to throw a few glances their way. The prisoners pulled picks and shovels from the rear of the second vehicle, an AUTONAV truck. They'd obviously been tasked with performing roadwork on the closed street. That wasn't what pulled my attention. Some wore orange jumpsuits. Others wore red and yellow.

I made my way along the base of the wall. It acted as a giant collector as the wind blew in bits of debris so my first garbage bag was soon full. When Picasso caught up with me, I asked him what the colors meant.

"Yellow is for cowards who used to support the Select but betrayed them," he whispered. "Pink jumpsuits are socialists, unionists or so-called journalists. The orange jumpsuits broke one or more of the old laws. Striped jumpsuits are for atheists stupid enough to declare themselves."

I'd seen yellow and pink jumpsuits only once. After the assassination, changes happened swiftly. Before the vice president was even sworn in as president, dozens of members of Congress were rounded up, each accused of participating in a vast conspiracy. Anyone who'd once suggested impeachment was a target. Federal investigations into the plot were truncated. The ruling party declared over and over, "Justice delayed is justice denied." They said vengeance on those who hated them had to be swift, before the rebels struck again.

The assassin was a sniper. The shooter was never found. Many in the opposition party disappeared in the night. After a week and a half, the propapundits finally reported that the politicians were missing. They seemed unconcerned. In fact, everyone on the news stated with certainty that Washington would work better without the obstructionists. The talking point became a drumbeat that entered every conversation: *When they come for you in a coup, you come for them in the night.*

After another few days, our new president admitted there had been mass arrests. If there were trials, they were held in secret. By the time the government went forward with the public hangings, torture had yielded all the confessions needed to proceed. The enemies of the state all wore jumpsuits at the executions, either yellow or striped.

As we watched the feed, Grammy told me not to look away at the moment the prisoners dropped. "Watch and learn," she said. "We thought it couldn't happen here but people are the same everywhere. It's happened before. We were foolish to think we were immune to the virus."

"The virus?"

"Potent combination." My grandmother pointed at the screening of the executions. "Fear and hate plus greed equal *that*."

Amid growing fears the new president would also be killed, the Select Few declared that democracy had to be suspended. The nation needed guidance "from power without one face."

The logic went that one man or woman could be assassinated but few Americans could even name the Select Few. Congress was dissolved. All government departments were corporatized (if they weren't already). The Select Few became our leaders so the government would be insulated from assassination threats, safe to rule as they saw fit.

The president ceded control and resigned. His speech was eloquent, soothing and, as Grammy put it, "complete horseshit."

The propapundits said the president would be kept on in an advisory role at a secure location. He was never seen or heard from again.

Responsibility for nuclear launch codes was given to a committee of generals, admirals and an unknown number of civilians chosen by the Select Few. Most people breathed a sigh of relief at that change. A unanimous vote was required before a nuclear strike could occur. We were assured that the public consensus agreed: A committee would be less likely to do — or achieve — much of anything, let alone use the nukes.

Which only goes to show a lot of people are idiots.

It wasn't an entirely smooth transition of power, of course. Many complained and protested. Opposition soon faded when the second round of mass arrests began. The speed of the collapse of the old system made little sense, but we soon became inured to the fact that old rules simply did not apply anymore. Phrases like *top secret*, *national security* and *safe transfer of power for the good of the country* were the only justifications needed to silence what critics remained.

Propapundits soothed us with pleas for calm and patience in what they called a time of correction. They claimed the death toll was exaggerated. Objections were argued and explained away as hysterical or treasonous.

People shrugged and began to sound like the Select's media representatives. Our own neighbors began to say things like, "The situation is fluid," and "The old ways failed to meet the challenges of the real world."

As we became used to the new normal, we forgot about the president. The world moved on. Some said our acceptance was cowardice. I think our capitulation was mostly due to fatigue. We were just trying to get by, day-to-day.

What anger remained was unfocused. It was true, the Select Few had no face. Our new leaders spoke to us through press releases. The propapundits parroted what they were told. The people were "resisting progress." A new American experiment had begun that would guarantee more freedoms, but only someday.

I was lost in those ugly memories when Picasso touched me on the shoulder. "Kismet? You okay?"

I nodded. "Yeah, why?"

"No matter what happens, stay away from the gate."

"What's going on?"

He pointed at his broken nose and grinned. "I got a nose for trouble. I think there might be some. An opportunity will present itself. Full moon's coming."

Before he turned away, I caught the worried look on Picasso's face. Though his leg gave him pain, he hurried back, limping awkwardly.

A very faint hum reached me. I looked back as a sleek low-slung red car arrived at Gate 27 from within the Circle. A young woman I could barely see through the darkened glass sat behind the steering wheel. She brushed her long blonde hair so aggressively it was obvious the car was in autonomous mode. The CSS officer stepped out of her shack, peered in the back of the car and waved at someone cheerily before hitting a button to raise the bar to allow passage.

As the car pulled into the street, several people yelled as one. I didn't catch the words but the tone was angry.

Two prisoners from the roadwork project tackled the centurion who held the rifle.

Four more charged the red car. One of them threw a spade like a spear and it bounced off the windshield, cracking and crinkling the safety glass.

The car screeched to a stop as two prisoners threw themselves before it.

The officer from the shack pulled a sidearm and began yelling for the rebels to get on the ground. The AUTONAV truck that had delivered the picks and shovels started up and made a quick tight turn. It was no longer autonomous. Picasso sat behind the wheel and drove the truck at high speed.

I gasped in horror as he aimed the vehicle at the CSS officer. The woman tried to step out of the way but the left front fender caught her in the shoulder.

I heard the crunch. My stomach turned and twisted. She sprawled on the pavement and was still. Her weapon spun away, skittered toward me. It came to rest not twenty feet away.

"Yee-haw!" Picasso screamed through his open window. "Let's take 'em to church! DHD!"

A white-haired man in a pink jumpsuit punctured one of the car's tires with one swing of his pickax. More prisoners descended on the vehicle and yelled for the woman to get out of her car. They rocked it back and forth violently.

My first instinct was to run. I didn't want to get into the middle of attempted murder, kidnapping and chaos. Rebellion was supposed to save lives and make things better. I wanted no part of this.

It wasn't the shouts of the angry prisoners that stirred my need to step in. A child was strapped in the back seat of that car, screaming in terror. Her fear was a call to action I could not refuse. The opportunity my sister and Chantelle had hinted at presented itself.

I scooped up the officer's pistol from the pavement as I rushed forward.

CHAPTER TWELVE

As I ran, I heard the first gunshot. The centurion with the rifle was short but he was thick through the chest and shoulders. Getting closer, I could see how strong he was. His arms bulged so much, his biceps may as well have been softballs. When two prisoners came for him, they tried to wrestle the weapon from his grasp.

The guard managed to twist the muzzle and turn the gun on a large man in an orange jumpsuit.

His attacker managed to say, "No," just before the guard pulled the trigger. The man went down.

The other attacker held on and, covered in hot blood, pleaded with other prisoners to save him. Three more — two men and a woman — rushed in. The officer was knocked to the ground, his weapon wrenched from his grasp. They could have taken him prisoner but instead tossed the rifle aside and began to stomp him.

The officers had failed to defend themselves or the people in the car. However, the melee served my purposes. The man with the pickax was about to drive it through the windshield when I put the handgun's muzzle to his bare neck.

The metal must have been cool against his hot skin. I could smell his stink and sweat as he stiffened and froze. Everyone slowed to a stop as if a great machine's gears were suddenly broken and winding down. The woman behind the wheel stopped screaming. Even the child quieted.

My target did not drop the pick. "You know how a gun works?" the prisoner asked.

"Why? Am I holding it backward?"

"There's a lot of us and only one of you," he rumbled.

He reminded me of Dobbs. He'd been too sure of himself, too. So sure he was dealing with a little girl who hadn't seen awful things. But I had seen awful things. I was ready for trouble.

"That pick in your hand is a tool," I told the prisoner. "You had to make it a weapon. What I've got? It's only good for one thing: turning you into a leaky bag of blood. I can take all y'all down before you can hurt me."

"You're a civilian. This isn't your business — "

"Child abuse is everybody's business. There's a kid in that car. Nobody here is a civilian but her."

One of the other prisoners yelled, "We don't have time for this. Stick to the plan!"

In the distance, sirens. Normally I would fear the wail of CSS vehicles rushing my way. However, the noise strengthened my resolve. "You said it. You don't have time for this. Run!"

A horn blared and I glanced to my right. Picasso sat behind the wheel of the truck. He blared the horn again and gestured frantically for the escapees to get in the back.

The horn and the sirens seemed to unstick the wheels of time and people started moving with purpose again. The prisoners who had attacked their captor dashed for the truck. That seemed to make the decision for those surrounding the little red car, as well. The white-haired man dropped his pick and ran for the truck. Prisoners were still jumping into the truck as Picasso began to pull away.

Not all the prisoners fled. Others stood behind the roadwork signs and watched them go. They glared at me but said nothing. One woman in a striped jumpsuit hurried to the fallen CSS officer and sat at his head, holding him still as she used her bare hand to compress a bleeding head wound.

Picasso disappeared around a corner in the stolen truck as CSS units arrived in patrol cars. The remaining prisoners sank to their knees and put their hands on top of their heads. Though their posture suggested they were resigned to their fate, they all continued to stare at me angrily.

My scalp was hot and my knees were weak. I couldn't seem to get enough air. It was as if the hot sun had burned some of the oxygen away and left me like a fish out of water, gasping and doomed.

"Put down the gun!"

The pistol was still in my hand but my arm was loose at my side. It wasn't pointing at anyone. That detail didn't matter. I wore a vest that identified me as a homeless person doing community service. Though I couldn't say precisely what my sin might be besides that of poverty, I was already guilty in the eyes of the Select and their agents.

Three guards trained their handguns on me. A fourth with a shotgun circled somewhere behind me. They all shouted at once. I dropped the pistol but their incomprehensible shouting did not cease.

I strained to understand their orders. One wanted me on my knees. Another screamed that I should flatten on the ground. Someone else told me to turn around. I closed my eyes and raised both arms, palms out to show them my hands were empty. "Don't shoot!" I said.

It's hard to sound calm and reasonable while at the same time trying to make yourself heard. Impossible, even. It did not escape my attention that one of the centurions, the one who yelled the loudest, was trembling and his finger was on the trigger. I felt like I was in a deadly game of Simon Says and bound to lose.

Another voice, high-pitched and young, joined me in shouting, "Don't shoot! Don't shoot her! She saved us!"

The little girl in the backseat of the car opened her door. Her voice alone was not enough but when she stepped out of the car, the officers all paused. They stopped shouting at me and began shouting at the child to stay away from me.

Then they shouted to each other. "Stand down! The kid is a Select!"

The guards advanced as one. The girl did not retreat. Instead, she threw her arms around me. That simple act probably saved my life.

I tried to keep my voice low, steady and reasonable as I addressed the men. "Two of yours are down." I nodded toward the still form of the woman on the ground. "She was hit by a truck. Call a medic. This gun belongs to her. I used it to stop the prisoners from taking these people in the car as hostages."

The CSS men converged on us, pulled the girl away and threw me to the ground. My left cheek ground into the pavement as a centurion knelt on my head. Another drove his knees into my back and twisted my arms behind me.

"Knife! She's got a knife!" one of them yelled. He almost sounded enthused. When they handcuffed me, I was sure they would find the other blade attached to my forearm so I told them it was there. I meant to assuage their fears but instead they pressed me harder into the ground.

I did not fight back. However, as was standard protocol, they kept shouting, "Stop resisting!"

Mama once told me that failure to use that procedure started a riot at a protest in Kansas City. Introducing that lie into the arrest gave the officers permission to use more violence and tended to give onlookers pause.

Flattened and struggling to breathe under their weight, I saw two other guards turn their attention to the centurion who'd been stomped. They pointed their pistols at the prisoner in the striped jumpsuit who'd run to the fallen man's aid.

The woman yelled, "He's hurt! I'm a nurse!"

She raised both arms to show her bloody hands were empty. Apparently, she moved too quickly or too slowly or not earnestly enough or ... something. One guard shot her twice in the chest. The other guard joined in. I'd heard of this before, too. Standard protocol: If one officer shoots, they all shoot. Failure to do so would get them in trouble with their superiors.

The nurse slumped to the ground with a thud and, in the sudden quiet, a collective moan of despair and disapproval rose from the prisoners who had elected to stay behind.

Someone still knelt on my head so I couldn't look away. I could have squeezed my eyes tight to block it all out but I knew I should watch. I watched the nurse bleed to death. It didn't take long. I'd seen death before, but not like this. The dead nurse wore the garb of an atheist yet she'd run to try to save her captor. She'd taken an oath that made her take action when a life was at stake.

I wondered if I should have ignored Sissy's plea for help. My parents had given me a mission, too: Stay with Grammy and take care of her. I was under arrest by ungrateful CSS officers who seemed determined to misunderstand the situation. At that moment, staying out of Atlanta seemed a better choice.

I wished that I could share Grammy's faith but I had a criminal secret. If the CSS could pry into my mind, they'd put me in a striped jumpsuit, too. As I wept for the murdered nurse, God's grace seemed pretty thin on the ground.

"Don't hurt her!" the little girl pleaded. "She didn't do anything wrong. She helped us. She stopped the bad people from getting us!"

Imagine being so young and naive to think that my innocence mattered. That one fresh thought alone made me weep a little harder. Though adults couldn't be trusted, the little girl was still innocent, achingly so.

The girl came into view and I got my first good look at her. She was blonde and blue-eyed and wore a frilly white dress. Her ballet slippers were pink. I'd seen pictures but I'd never seen such things in person. I guessed she was nine.

The CSS officer who'd been kneeling on me got off as the girl squatted to look me in the eyes. She smiled and said, "Don't worry. I won't let them hurt you anymore. My name is Eileen but everybody calls me Eye. What's your name?"

That's how I met the only angel I'll ever believe in.

For a few seconds, I had a glimmer of hope. That light was extinguished as the guards pulled a black bag over my head.

CHAPTER THIRTEEN

The CSS agents tossed me into the back of a truck roughly. They seemed to hit every bump and take every corner fast. Sweat stung my eyes and my breath came fast as I was slammed into the walls of my mobile prison. With the handcuffs pulled tight and blind to my surroundings, it was nearly impossible to protect myself. By the time the vehicle finally stopped, I felt battered and bruised.

I lay there for a while, I'm not sure how long. I was beginning to suspect I'd been forgotten when they came for me.

At least two guards grabbed me. They said nothing. Someone with large rough hands searched me again but it seemed more like an opportunity to grope me. The hood stayed on my head. I remained silent so as not to provoke my captors.

Once that horror was complete, they marched me into a building. I was indoors so I doubted I'd been sent to a detention camp. Judging from the echoes of moans and shouts ringing off the walls, I was in some sort of holding facility. The prisoners were restless which suggested to me they were either new to jail or had been incarcerated so long they were past worrying about annoying the authorities.

Someone shoved me from behind and a metal door slammed. Carefully, moving slowly, I determined my surroundings by edging into things. A table stood in the middle of the room, two chairs on one side and one chair on the other.

An interrogation room, I thought.

I strained to hear something but could only detect the sound of my hot breaths within the hood. By the deadness in the room, I suspected it was soundproofed.

Bad news. Not an interrogation room. I'm in a place where prisoners are made to shout things others aren't meant to hear. They torture people here.

I pulled the chair out from the table with my foot and sat down. I listened for another few minutes to make sure no one else was in the room. It was a good bet a camera's eye was on me but I was alone for the moment. Only then did I allow the tears to flow. I tried not to sob or let a single moan escape in case the CSS was listening.

I'd heard stories of places like this from refugees traveling through Campbellford. CSS would leave people alone with their fear for a while to soften them up. They'd deny the relief of a trip to the bathroom until all their questions were answered.

Refugees said the CSS used fire hoses on prisoners who lost bowel or bladder control. Sometimes they'd blast cold water to make you scream and pee yourself just to blame you for making a mess.

One traveler, a woman from Louisville who'd come by Grammy's gate, said the torture technique had a name: pressure washing. "The water comes at you hard, near enough to skin you. Then they leave you in wet clothes and turn up the cold air in the room. If you complain about that, they cut off all your clothes and laugh at you. Maybe more than laugh. Hard to say what's the worst of it," she added. "I guess it's all the worst of it. There are no good parts."

Protocol strikes again, I thought. How many casual cruelties went unexamined because "that's the way it's done"?

I heard the heavy steel door open on creaking hinges and quickly slam shut. Listening carefully, I could tell it was a large man. His footsteps and his breathing were heavy. He circled me twice and I heard a subtle clicking sound.

After another moment, he stood behind me. The clicking continued and several nightmarish possibilities raced through my mind. I doubted it was a pen. Was it a switchblade? I didn't think so but why stand behind me that long? Was he building up his nerve before delivering a beating to soften me up for interrogation?

I hunched in my seat, squeezed my eyes tight and braced for the first blow, keeping my mouth closed and my jaw set, hoping I wouldn't lose any teeth.

The hood was whipped off my head and I blinked at the sudden bright light. The oldest centurion I'd ever seen limped around to the side of the table so I could see him. He held a remote control in his hand. He pointed to the wall opposite me. It was a freeze-frame of surveillance from Gate 27. The picture showed me picking up the gun.

He advanced the recording frame by frame until I was shown pointing the pistol at the prisoner with the pickax. "That you?"

Of course, it was. I nodded.

"Speak up for the record, girl."

"Yes. I am Kismet Beatriz and that is a picture of me rescuing that kid."

"Why?"

I shrugged. "It seemed like the right thing to do. "

"Seemed like?"

"The way you guys are treating me, I'm not so sure anymore."

"Who put you up to it?"

"No one."

"So you just happened to be in the right place at the right time?"

"Seems like wrong place, wrong time to me."

"You say things seem like this and seem like that. I don't like weasel words when I ask a question."

"I can only tell you what I know and I don't know anything."

"You claim no advance knowledge of the kidnapping attempt?"

"I'm not claiming it. I'm saying it. That much, I do know."

"And what reward do you expect for this selfless act of heroism?"

"Nothing," I said. "And I didn't feel brave. I just felt like I had to — "

"Because you had to save the little girl and her nanny?"

I took a deep breath. "It's apparent you don't believe me so let's look at it from your cynical point of view — "

He corrected me, "Skeptical. I'm skeptical."

"Fine. I was already standing there. If the kidnapping happened and I did nothing, I'd be in trouble for that, right?"

"We have to investigate subjects. When it comes to cases involving the Select, we take our questions and your answers very seriously, Miss *Beatriz* — "

I didn't like the extra emphasis he put on my last name. It sounded like an accusation, as if he was trying to make my name sound like a bad word.

"If I did nothing, I'd be in this chair and you'd still be treating me like shit, right?"

"Where crimes against the Select are involved, we accept no so-called witnesses at face value."

"Little wonder you have so few witnesses when bad things happen."

"Insolence won't get you far, Miss."

"Maybe not ... but heroism sure hasn't helped much, either."

"I'll ask again: You expect no reward from the Select Few?"

"All I want is to get out of here."

"So you swear you're not a social climber?"

"I wouldn't know how."

The old centurion stared at me for a few awkward seconds before giving a tiny, almost imperceptible nod. He stepped behind me. I expected to get hit and for the questioning to continue. Instead, he yanked the black hood down over my head again.

I heard one more click and then his heavy footsteps, the opening and slamming of the steel door. Alone again, I waited.

Blind and bound, I was at the mercy of Citizen Security and Safety. They were not known for their mercy.

My hope was dwindling but I finally had my answer for the refugee from Louisville. The worst things about being a prisoner were not all equal. Skin can heal. Wounds may close. The humiliation of the arrest would stay with me. It was powerlessness that made me weep, though. Helplessness was the worst of it.

Exhaustion seeped into my marrow but I could not sleep. Time passed but not enough that I could grow bored of my dread.

CHAPTER FOURTEEN

The cuffs were so tight my hands tingled. Then they went numb. I wanted to scream but I held back. This was my time to wait, listen and learn. For the risk I was taking, there would be no acknowledgment unless my mission was a total success.

My respect for people in uniform had been ingrained in me. The way CSS manhandled me and abused their power, that feeling drained away. To keep us scared, CSS methods were brutal. In their hearts, they must have known they were weak and afraid.

The door opened and shut and two people entered. Someone circled, stalking me on heavy heels. The chair opposite me was pulled back, its metal feet scraping on the concrete floor. I had nothing to tell them about the escaped prisoners that could be of use. I wondered if there was a drain in the floor. Maybe this was the room where they used the fire hose. Would they take their time working up to that? The interrogation would escalate quickly if I disappointed them and that seemed inevitable.

A guard yanked the hood from my head. I winced as a bright light shone in my eyes. He put his mouth so close to my ear, I could smell the synth beer and fake meat on his hot breath. "Behave."

He made for the exit and, as he opened the door, someone screamed. There were no words, just anguish. Whether the pain was mental or physical, I couldn't be sure. As the door closed, we were plunged once more into silence.

The light in my face clicked off and I found the person across the table was a middle-aged woman. The shoulders of her pinstripe suit were padded. Her hair was piled high in a gravity-defying hairstyle. She was pretty but the look on her face was severe. It was her lips that drew my gaze. Rather than drawing lipstick across them, she'd painted a dot in the middle. I'd seen that color on a discarded soda can once: blood orange.

"Kismet Beatriz." She spoke my name in a British accent. Ordinarily, that might have been pleasant. However, in her mouth, my name obviously tasted sour. "My name is Evelyn Rossi. You had quite an adventure this morning, didn't you?"

I said nothing. Instead, I memorized her face. If I ever got out of here, I wanted to be sure to know the face of my enemies.

"I've seen the surveillance recording of what happened at Gate 27, Kismet. I also watched the video of you speaking to the man who drove the truck that took the escaped prisoners away."

"Then you know I did nothing wrong. I barely spoke to him."

"I'm referring to the surveillance camera at the shelter. You stood in line at the soup kitchen for quite some time. He seemed very friendly to you. You spoke to a couple, as well. The authorities are still searching for those two. This could go very well for you if you answer correctly. It will go even better if you omit any lies you are contemplating."

"The boy in the line tried to pick me up. I wasn't interested. We just passed the time. I don't even remember what that couple talked about. They were just somebody at the shelter, that's all."

Evelyn indicated a camera high up on a far wall. "Your answers are still being recorded. They want to know the name of the man in line, the one who drove the getaway vehicle."

Picasso, I thought. *What have you gotten me into?*

I guessed that the shelter had video surveillance but, with all the crowds at the shelter, it seemed unlikely they possessed audio. "He never told me his name."

"Really?"

"I don't recall that he did. You know how it is. A stranger tells you his name and unless you are interested and commit it to memory, the name flies away a second later. Don't you have his identity from the bio-scan?"

"Bio-scans can be faked."

"I didn't know that."

"It's happened before."

"I wouldn't know about that."

My ignorance seemed to satisfy her. "Let's talk about you. The happenings at Gate 27 were interesting. Your actions left me wondering about your motivations."

I shrugged. What reply could I offer that might satisfy her? Judging from my treatment thus far, the CSS had decided I was guilty of something.

"You didn't know the boy in line was part of an escape plan?"

"If I'd known I would have gotten off the truck and done my sanitation duty somewhere else. I didn't want to be within miles of all that."

"The guards will recover from their wounds," Evelyn said. It seemed the dead nurse who tried to help was of no consequence. "The truck was found abandoned a few streets away."

"As far as I can guess, the guy I spoke to — the guy who spoke to me — might have acted on impulse."

"Doubtful. The vest he wore from the shelter was found in an alley. Someone was waiting with bolt cutters." She pointed at the green vest I still wore. "It's the devil getting out of those things without an authorized guard."

"This is my first time in one of these vests. It's not my color."

"Don't try to be funny," Evelyn warned. "This is not a time for jokes, especially lame ones. It's bad form. I absolutely *abhor* bad form."

"Noted, ma'am."

"What are you, eighteen?

"Twenty."

"And new to the city, I understand."

"Last night was my first in Atlanta."

"You found trouble quickly."

"Trouble found me."

"When you were arrested, you had two combat knives on you."

"I'm a woman traveling alone. I should be armed to the teeth."

"But you picked up a CSS officer's weapon."

"I wasn't looking to make it a fair fight, ma'am."

She allowed herself a small smile but that faded quickly. "You expect me to believe that you somehow stumbled into the middle of a prison break on your first day here?"

"There's trouble all over, isn't there? It's easy to step in manure in a field fertilized with it."

"I told you not to try to be funny."

"Just something my grandmother would say."

"Biometrics tells us you belong in a little town from up north I've barely heard of."

"Campbellford. I don't belong there, either."

Evelyn reached down. She must have had a purse or a case with her. When she sat up, she held a cigar and, after much puffing and sucking, lit it. She blew a smoke ring. "I get these from the New Cuban Republic, Kismet. They are quite a treat. Cigars are my luxury. You seem to be indulging in a luxury, as well. Can you guess what that might be?"

"From where I sit, I can't think of a single one, ma'am."

"Your luxury is a delusion of grandeur. You think you don't belong where you came from."

"I left Grammy and came to Atlanta to look for work."

"Long way to come. Why not look somewhere else?"

"Everywhere else is farther."

Evelyn blew another perfect ring of smoke. She looked relaxed but I suspected she was playing for time, gathering her thoughts before coming at me again. "Your 'grammy,' hm? Quaint."

"I'd say sweet."

"Don't contradict me, girl. If I say it's quaint, that's what it is. Where are your parents?"

"Both career military." I looked at the floor and blinked away a tear. "Duty called them elsewhere."

She sighed and I had the impression Evelyn would rather be somewhere else, too. "So you claim no knowledge. You had no warning of what was coming despite the fact that you were with the driver of the truck who helped the prisoners escape. You had no ulterior motives or expectation of a reward when you stepped in to stop the men who damaged the red car?"

"I had no foreknowledge whatsoever, no. You talk like I had time to think about it. I didn't. I heard the little girl screaming and I couldn't stand it. I had to stop them to protect her."

"You seem very well-spoken. You can read, can't you?"

"Read, write, type, skip rope, sure."

"How does a homeless girl who sleeps in a shelter know a word like 'foreknowledge?'"

"I'm an educated fool, I guess. My mother was hurt in the Middle East. An IED took her left leg. She was on medical leave for a long time. Grammy's got no use for proper grammar but when Mama was home, I was homeschooled. My parents were educated — "

"In the military?"

"No, they met in the military. My father went to Boston University. My mother attended McGill." I hastened to add, "before the Water Wars." All this information could be gleaned from my biometric record but I sensed Evelyn doubted me.

"How did your father get the money to get an education at BU?"

"My grandfather on Daddy's side owned a furniture business in Boston. My mother's father was in the import/export business, mostly drugs from Canada. The crash killed the furniture business and the embargo and the Water War threw Mama's dad into bankruptcy."

Evelyn straightened. She seemed to look at me in a new light. "These businesses ... they were successful before?"

"Granddaddy owned four furniture stores and a carpet store. Papa Bear had a big house in New Brunswick and a bigger house in Boston. When the border closed, he was on the wrong side. We haven't had any messages from him since. He was old. He's probably dead by now."

"You might have been a Select — "

"Oh, my grandparents were well off but we were never *that* rich."

"Do not interrupt me."

"Sorry."

"And do not refer to the Select as rich or wealthy. That's coarse and inaccurate. The Select Few are *blessed*. Perhaps your grandparents would have done better had they not fallen from grace."

I bristled. "Bad luck, is all."

"Believing in luck, good or bad, is one of the ways people fall from grace.

Evelyn's chair scraped the floor as she stood and turned to the surveillance camera. "I have all I need. Unless there is something else for you, cut her loose. She doesn't know anything useful about anything."

I was nothing more than an insect that had somehow found my way into her house.

"Kismet, I would suggest you return to your grandmother in your little village and, like Lot's wife, maybe you better not look back."

I shook my head. "Good advice. Can't take it. Gotta find a job, ma'am."

Evelyn took another long drag from her cigar. "I have two additional questions. First, about confronting those men, would you do the same again, given the choice?"

"That kid was scared. I don't want to be the kind of person who would ignore something like that. It's not about having a choice. My reaction bypassed thought."

"Reactions that bypass thought are often dangerous. Dumb people bypass thought all the time."

"Do you think saving that child was dumb?"

She ignored my question. "Tell me, what is your greatest fear, Kismet?"

I searched for one answer among too many possibilities and settled on the most personal and truthful. "That I'm not enough, or will never be enough."

Evelyn took a long drag and blew another perfect smoke ring. "That's a good answer. You're right to fear that. You will never be enough."

Tears welled in my eyes. "Are you done with me?"

"I have a job for you."

"I don't want to be a spy for CSS."

Evelyn laughed. "I don't work for them. They work to serve and protect me and my family." She glared at the surveillance camera and, when she spoke with heat, her British accent slipped a little. "Which they very nearly failed to do!"

"You're Eileen's mother?" I asked.

"I stand among the Select Few now but I've been where you are. What you could never understand is a person in my position. People are always begging, demanding more of us. Everyone wants something and no one does anything for selfless reasons. And yet here you are, saving my daughter without a thought in your head. That sort of empty-headedness approaches sainthood these days."

"Thanks ... I think."

"I must seem harsh to you but I have to be careful about social climbers. You can't be one of them. You have no guile. Your brain was elsewhere but your heart was in the right place. You are salvageable."

"I'm dizzy from all these compliments!"

She smiled. "Conspiracies are beyond you but everyone wants something. Tell me, what is it you really want? Name your selfish desire."

"A place to sleep and regular hot meals."

Evelyn was pretty but her smile was not. "Gloriously low expectations. How simple your life must be. How happy you must be."

"Not so far. Outside the wall, regular meals and a safe place to sleep are hard to come by. You say you've been in my position. Maybe you've forgotten some of it."

She laughed. "For rescuing my daughter, you have my sincere thanks. You can continue to look out for my daughter. Maybe you can skip rope with her. Eye likes that."

"I ... accept."

Evelyn pinned me in my seat with an intense gaze. "You did something without thought that was over in seconds. I owe you for that. To be clear, though, I'm taking you on for a commitment that should last a long time if you do well by me. You're getting this chance because of one well-spent minute of your life. My investment in you could last years. You owe *me*. Understood?"

Evelyn didn't wait for my answer. Instead, she spun on her heel to leave. "When they let you out, wait out front. I'll send someone to pick you up. I have to get back. Eye has been *so* traumatized by all this, it's absolutely unconscionable."

So it wasn't an interrogation. It was a job interview.

CHAPTER FIFTEEN

As I stepped out of the cold detention center, humidity enveloped me so quickly and completely the effect was claustrophobic. I was still trembling as sweat trickled down my neck.

I'd only been away for days but it already felt like weeks. Was Grammy pestering Lisa for my whereabouts, wondering when I'd return to Campbellford? The better question was, would I ever get back?

As I shook my tingling hands and rubbed my wrists to get the circulation back, an electric blue pickup truck pulled up beside me. The old woman at the wheel wore a dark blue visor to shield her eyes and a red apron with white pinstripes. She'd been a brunette but was now mostly gray. I guessed she was in her late 70s. Her hair was piled high, much as Evelyn Rossi's had been. I wondered if that was the common style within New Atlanta.

"I'm looking for a girl by the name of Kismet. That you?"

"Yes."

"If true, what's your last name?"

"Beatriz."

She nodded and unlocked the doors. "I'm Wanda. Get in."

I climbed in beside her and she sped off. "Mrs. Rossi wanted to know if CSS had any more questions for you."

"No, they seemed to leave all that to her. If I didn't know better, I'd guess the CSS is a little afraid of Evelyn."

"Mostly respect, I suspect. She came up from nothin' and now she's Captain of the Guard. And that's Mrs. Rossi to you."

"Mrs. Rossi, then. I had no idea of her rank. Her English accent sure threw me — "

"*Sh!* She can talk whatever way she likes."

"I'm trying to understand so I don't make mistakes in front of them."

"Too many questions are not healthy."

"I thought the CSS handled all policing and I wondered if her accent was real and — "

I'd been in the truck for less than two minutes. Wanda gave a long-suffering sigh as if I'd been bothering her all my life. "Citizen Security and Safety is for everything outside the wall. Different rules inside the Circle. You'll learn all this as you go. Listen more than you talk, always. You're in high cotton now so you better start acting like it if you expect to last."

"Isn't it strange that not even one CSS detective had any questions for me, though?"

She shook her head. "Not strange at all if you know who really runs this town. Besides, they know who they're after. It's not like they're going to have a trial after they catch up with those runners."

"I suppose not."

"The Select Few banish climbers and shoot spies. I hear you were armed when you were arrested. It's dangerous to have a weapon on you when you're arrested. You're lucky to be alive."

"The bastards kept my knives."

"No rough talk. If Mrs. Rossi hears any foul language around Eye, you're gone. As for your weapons, Mrs. Rossi has them. You'll get the knives back when you leave her employ."

"They told me they were keeping my weapons and my backpack."

"I hope you didn't make too much of a fuss. They were messing with you."

"They did laugh a lot as I walked out the door."

"CSS agents aren't paid particularly well. They have to get their fun where they can."

I thought again about the rough hands that had groped me when I'd arrived at their jail. I could still feel where I'd been mauled, sore places. I cursed under my breath.

I didn't know what to do with my hands. Whenever I felt nervous, holding the grips of my parents' combat knives made me feel a little better. My father's knife made me feel strong. My mother's blade made me feel lucky. When I touched the hair clip Chantelle had given me, I felt no solace, only danger.

Wanda glanced away from the road to look me up and down. "Skinny little thing, aren't ya? You eaten?"

I hadn't eaten anything since the shelter that morning. It was early evening and I was ravenous. Wanda pointed at the basket between us. "Have a couple of carrots. That'll fill you up for now. Not more than two, mind. I'm making borscht tonight. You're in luck tomorrow. I got hold of some cornmeal so I'm making polenta. You know what that is?"

"No."

"Everybody loves my polenta. I call it my job security meal. Nobody makes it as good as me."

The carrots looked like dirty twisted thumbs. I began to brush them off. Wanda told me not to soil her truck. "You gotta eat a pecka dirt before you die. It's good for you, minerals and whatnot. Have a chaw and a gnaw."

Too hungry to be too fussy, I ate. "I take it you're the Rossi's cook?"

"Chief cook and bottle washer, yeah. The carrots are good, huh?"

"Thank you."

She nodded as if I'd passed a test known only to her. "Just came from the shelter."

"Oh? Why?"

"Commoners come in the front. Servants of the Circle go in the back and get first pick."

"I don't understand. Why would anyone from New Atlanta need to get rations from a homeless shelter?"

Wanda rolled her eyes. "You're a lamb fresh from the farm. Our betters eat well. We're staff. Our dinners are subsidized."

"Subsidized by a homeless shelter."

"You woke up homeless and tonight I'm cookin' for you. Be grateful."

"I just didn't think anyone on the other side of that wall would be one step up from homeless."

"Life's simple back on that farm, huh, little lamb? There's all kinds of steps up and down. At the bottom are refugees, then comes homeless and that's just the beginning. Being a person of means is the main thing. After that? A lot depends on how white you are. By the looks of you, you shouldn't put on airs or get any fancy ideas. You won't find any other girls named Kismet among the blessed but, if you play your cards right, you can find shelter in the shadows."

"Sounds cold, out of the sun. Where are you on the ladder, Wanda?"

"I got my polenta goin' for me and I've been with the Rossi family since Mr. Rossi was a boy."

"What does he do?"

"Do? About what?"

"They're Select, so where's their money come from?"

Wanda seemed to consider her words carefully. "The Rossi family is a dynasty. Mr. Rossi's great-grandfather was big in the cotton business, his grandfather was big in the lumber business. Mr. Rossi's father, the man who hired me when I wasn't much older than you are now, was a hedge fund manager. Your employer's name is Kirk Rossi but it will always be Mr. Rossi to you. He spends most of his days managing the family fortune. So you know, that's more than you need to know. Our jobs are to facilitate the small things so the family can attend to the big things."

"He manages money and she's head of security behind the wall?"

"Mrs. Rossi started out as an AWE agent and caught his eye. You may have noticed she's quite the looker."

"AWE? What's that?"

"You don't know anything, do you?"

"Maybe not but I pick up things quick."

"Was that sass? I don't need your sass."

"I'm just trying to live and learn, Wanda."

She stopped the truck and eyed me for a few seconds. "Mrs. Rossi said you were an educated fool. Eileen could use that but I don't want her to learn any sass back, you understand? Eye is a pure spirit and we don't want to mess that up. She'll rule the world someday."

"Mrs. Rossi told me I'm to take care of Eye. I'm not great at math but I've been told I have a large vocabulary."

"Uh-huh. 'Pride goeth before destruction and a haughty spirit before a fall,' Kismet. Proverbs 16:18. I'm not much for recitin', but to stay in Mrs. Rossi's good graces, get ready to hear some Bible quotes. Be a good listener. Your best bet is always silence. That's what Mrs. Rossi most enjoys from servants." Wanda put the truck in gear and we were in motion again.

"You remind me of my grandmother, Wanda."

"Yeah? That's nice, I guess."

I loved my grandmother but Grammy had her foul moods, especially when her arthritis flared up.

"About your first responsibility, the child likes to be called Eye," Wanda told me. "That's just for now. She's only twelve."

"Really? She's small for twelve. I thought she was younger."

"She was born premature. Eileen entered this world early but New Atlanta has the best hospital in this hemisphere. So many nights I stayed up, rocking that baby to sleep. The pregnancy was difficult. There will be no more heirs for Mr. and Mrs. Rossi. That makes little Eileen a very fortunate girl. She will be American royalty. When she's sixteen, you'll be calling her Miss Rossi, as will I. That's if you last that long." Wanda gave me a hard look. "The girl you're replacing didn't last more than a few months."

"Oh?"

"You've met her."

"Have I?"

"Tanya Dunford," Wanda explained. "Don't say that name in the house or Mrs. Rossi will toss a fit and have another of her headaches."

"I don't know any Tanya Dunford."

"The girl at the wheel of the red Tesla this morning. Mrs. Rossi wanted her head on a spike. When those prisoners attacked the car, I hear she was useless. Didn't get Eye out of danger, just sat at the wheel and screamed."

"I don't remember her screaming," I said.

"Tanya wasn't a bad girl but she was about as useful in that situation as an umbrella at the bottom of a lake. Mr. and Mrs. Rossi are livid about the car. Do you know how hard it is to get hold of parts in this day and age? Fixing that machine is going to cost a fortune."

I gave Wanda a few minutes of silence before I dared to ask another question. "So ... in the interest of being educated instead of just an educated fool, what is AWE? In case Eye asks me questions, so I know what not to say?"

Posing the question that way appealed to Wanda. "A division of Inner Circle Security. CSS jurisdiction ends at the wall. AWE stands for Always Watching Everywhere. It's the surveillance arm of the company."

"Company? So ... mercenaries?"

"That's impolite. Think of it as the Select Few's private army. Mrs. Rossi was a pilot in the Air Force before she joined AWE. She started out here as a parrot."

"A what?"

Wanda smiled for the first time. "You ever call her that, she'll use your own knives on you. The wall has towers and parapets. They call AWE sentries parrots because they're up there in their perches. Your home is New Atlanta now. The wall is the Circle and it's what makes the Select Few possible. Climbers are massing in Old Atlanta, looking our way with envious eyes. That's why the parrots are always watching everywhere. Surveillance is everywhere."

For a fleeting second, Wanda pointed at the truck's dashboard. It was the most subtle of warnings that even at that moment, someone could be listening.

"The world is not a safe place," Wanda continued. "Today Eye got her first real glimpse of how dangerous it really is. Until this morning, she was an untouchable princess, safe in her fairytale castle."

The wall was a blur, zipping by on our right. Behind it, several glass high-rises towered like uneven teeth against the darkening sky. The

Circle made for an intimidating fortress. As we approached a gate to enter New Atlanta, Wanda's words came back to me and this time they sounded pleasingly ironic. "Pride goeth before destruction and a haughty spirit before a fall."

There were micro-fractures in the foundation of their barrier to reality. Sissy's mission for me was to turn those tiny cracks into fissures.

CHAPTER SIXTEEN

We approached the gate at dusk — number 27 — the same place where I'd been an unwelcome outsider that morning. The little red car had been towed away. Two small AUTONAV trucks were ahead of us in line to enter the Circle. A gate of steel mesh raised and lowered before each vehicle could advance.

"They're on higher alert now," Wanda muttered. "It's a bother. AWE is on the lookout for spies all the time but they're more uptight now. They consider going after the daughter of the Captain of the Guard impolite. Mrs. Rossi was in the Security Center most of the day scanning surveillance recordings inside and outside the Circle. They will catch those escaped prisoners and anyone who helped or harbored them."

Good luck, Picasso, I thought. *Run far, run fast. Vaya con Dios.*

As we paused at the gate, a CSS officer scanned Wanda's face. It was a formality since it was obvious he recognized her. However, when he scanned my face, the guard's brow furrowed. He put a hand on his sidearm as he ordered me to get out of the truck.

"Hold on, Baxter!" Wanda called out in an amiable tone. "She's new to the house of Rossi. Call before this gets out of hand. Her name is Kismet Beatriz. She must not be in the system yet."

House of Rossi? I suppressed a smirk. I sat on the border of a foreign country whose ways were strange and exotic.

The guard reached for his radio instead of his handgun and made the call. After a moment's consultation, he told us to wait as he retreated into his shack.

I peered through the gate to get my first glimpse of what lay beyond the wall. I'd pictured large estate homes. What I found instead was a crowded city street not so different from the rest of Atlanta. The first business I saw inside the circle was a Starbucks. I'd heard of them but I'd never seen one. I had no idea such remnants of the Old World still existed and I told Wanda so.

"Makes sense, doesn't it?" Wanda groused. "When the Crash hit, everyone suddenly realized they were poor. Fancy drinks faded a bit after that."

"But they're still a thing here."

"The Select can afford it."

"I never asked," I said hesitantly. "As a servant in the high house of Rossi, what will my salary be?"

She shrugged. "You'll take what they give you and you'll be happy about it. Just don't expect to be swigging down espresso drinks at that coffee shop, okay?"

"Whatever I make, I need to send most of it to my grandmother."

Wanda glanced my way. "I'm sure Mr. Rossi can arrange that for you. I don't mean to pry but your grandmother, she got troubles?"

"Yes." I looked away so she wouldn't see the tears welling in my eyes.

To my right, a familiar stranger stood alone in the gathering gloom. There were a few other people on the street but she pulled my attention because she was the only one standing still. She stared at the gate.

No, not at the gate. At me.

I rolled down my window and leaned forward to get a better look. She was too far away for me to be certain. I felt a wave of discomfort cresting at the edges of perception. Did she emanate fear? Was the fear all mine? Was this a warning and from what quarter would the danger come? I couldn't be sure.

I wanted to call out to her and perhaps she sensed it. Or maybe she just wanted me to know how she felt. The figure quickly turned and strode away.

The guard emerged from his shack and gave us the nod to proceed. "Kismet Beatriz, you're in the system now." He said it as if I'd won a prize. I suppose in a way I had.

As we rolled through Gate 27 and inside the Circle, I asked, "Wanda, you said I replaced Eye's nanny."

"Tanya, yes."

"What will happen to her?"

Wanda was quiet for a moment. I wasn't sure she was going to answer. Finally, she said, "Banished. She's out of New Atlanta for good and she won't be coming back. I get the feeling you have a soft heart, Kismet. Harden it a little. There are dangers on either side of the gate. She might be safer than you are now. Watch your step."

I closed my eyes and pictured the young woman. Maybe she'd sleep in a crowded shelter and working off her breakfast somewhere in the city the next morning. Whatever became of my predecessor, the quick and casual way she lost her place within the Circle served as a dire warning.

"Never drop your guard or allow yourself to get comfortable among those people," Sissy had cautioned me. "Until the war is over, you have no friends you can trust."

A day that had begun with a man coughing himself to death in a homeless shelter had tilted from chaos and violence in the street to the horrors of arrest, mistreatment, and captivity. As Wanda drove me toward my new home, I should have been relieved.

As we waited for the steel gate to rise, a sign ahead of us glowed bright yellow: *May the Circle be unbroken. Welcome to the Future!*

Then the sign blinked to read in bright red: *See something? Say something. Always Watching Everywhere in full effect.*

I'd changed places with Evelyn Rossi's servant. Instead, I felt as if I'd swallowed a stone. Some days you just want to crawl into a hole and pull it in behind you. That was how I felt as I entered the realm of the Select Few.

CHAPTER SEVENTEEN

New Atlanta was labyrinthine, like the inside of an anthill. Instead of a grid, the streets wound and curled in hairpin turns around high-rises and gigantic mansions. If there was an order to the city within a city, I couldn't detect it. My new home was a drunk libertarian's dream of design. As I thought about it, the layout reflected New Atlanta's founders. If the Select Few had a motto it might be, "You can't tell me what to do!"

The speed limit seemed more appropriate for navigating a crowded parking garage. I was reminded of the American base in Bermuda. The tiny island was made larger by a slow speed limit. It seemed to take a long time to get anywhere, but time meant less then. Mama was flirting with a medical discharge. We had a few empty days to spend, paid for with pain. For once, we were well-fed and unhurried.

I stayed at that base through most of her recovery. Though she'd lost a leg, our time there was the happiest of my childhood. The library was well-stocked and when she wasn't working in physiotherapy getting used to her new prosthesis, we spent our time reading on beaches of pink sand. On my final night on the island, I wept.

"Don't cry, Kismet," Mama said. "I'm well enough to go back to work so that's what I have to do. Besides, Grammy misses you."

"I'm gonna miss you," I told her. The memory made me tear up a little.

Wanda slid a glance my way. "Feeling overwhelmed?"

I was supposed to be impressed by what the Select had created. Instead, I asked, "Is there, like, a business district and a residential area or is it sort of all over the place?"

"This is the home of the Select Few," Wanda replied sourly. "Everything is business, even the golf course. Especially the golf course, or so I'm told. I've never been."

"Beijing had the Forbidden City," I said. "They called it that because no one could enter or leave without the permission of the Emperor."

"The Circle's full of emperors. You need to concern yourself with the permission of three people: Mr. Rossi, Mrs. Rossi and little old me."

"Yes, ma'am."

"Call me Wanda, not ma'am. Every-damn-body calls me Wanda. Titles of any kind aren't for common people. Don't want anyone thinking I'm putting on airs."

Was Wanda always so humble or did working for the Select demand humility? From what I knew of Evelyn Rossi, I'd entered a place that demanded unquestioning servility. That sounded terrible but it wasn't so very different from anywhere else.

Darkness came a little earlier within the Select's walls. By the time we made our way through those narrow winding streets, I was ravenous again. It couldn't have been far to the Rossi's home but every route seemed circuitous. I was later to learn that the only straight streets within the circle were around the big stores and the armory. The autonomous trucks required more room and wider passages to deliver their goods.

The Rossi house was taller than most single residences I'd seen, five stories. It seemed almost everything was new within the Circle but the narrowness of their home made me think of a nursery rhyme my father taught me.

There was a crooked man who walked a crooked mile.
He found a crooked sixpence against a crooked stile.
He bought a crooked cat which caught a crooked mouse
and they all lived together in a crooked little house.

Daddy said there was a serious story behind the silly rhyme. It was about how people in Scotland and England found a way to live together peacefully. Mama laughed at that and told him not to fill my head with stories that weren't really true and never would be. Mama taught me facts. Daddy taught me to dream.

I wondered what they'd say if they could see me arriving at the Rossi home. I guessed that Daddy would tell me he believed in me, that everything would work out. Mama would warn me to keep a blade close by. "Just in case, because you know how people are. Remember Dobbs."

The narrow driveway snaked around the back of the house and into an underground parking garage. There was enough space for four vehicles: Wanda's pickup, a blue sedan, and a long white limousine. One space was empty, probably for the sporty red car Tanya had driven into trouble.

As I got out of the truck, I looked around and tried to marry the wide dimensions of the garage with the narrowness of the house above us. I mentioned my confusion to Wanda.

"The Rossis own the houses on either side of this one. There's a short tunnel that ties all three. I'll let Eye give you the full tour tomorrow. I'm sure she'd enjoy showing off."

"*Three* houses?" That struck me as an extravagance that was not just foreign. This was an alien culture.

My surprise must have shown on my face. Wanda explained, "The CSS has their centurions but AWE is elite, Mrs. Rossi's praetorian guard."

"I don't really know what that's supposed to mean."

"That's the problem with your generation: no future, no sense of history, either."

She pointed to her left. "That door leads to the Rossi's private home which you'll be allowed to clean if you're good."

Wanda pointed at a steel door with a key card lock. "That's the Circle's Security and Surveillance Center."

"Convenient for Mrs. Rossi, I guess."

"Precisely," Wanda whispered. "The only way to get in there is to wear a uniform ... or maybe sneak in, I suppose. Up to you."

I smiled weakly.

"First things first: I've got boxes of vegetables in the back of the truck. Your first official service will be carting them upstairs for me."

As I went around to the back of the truck I risked another glance at the door to the Security Center. A surveillance camera sat above the steel door. Without a key card, there seemed no way to get through. And how many AWE guards worked in the rooms beyond?

That was a problem. On the other side of that door was where I needed to be.

CHAPTER EIGHTEEN

The decor inside what I came to call the narrow house was dark, cramped, old-fashioned and littered with antiques. I was cutting up beets in the kitchen when I met the master of the house, Kirk Rossi.

He was a tall, thin man of about thirty-five with thinning sandy hair. He stood at a distance in the small dining room for some time before approaching me. I said nothing and went about my work under Wanda's direction. He must have preferred to watch me before announcing his presence. By the time he emerged from my peripheral vision and entered the kitchen, I was already annoyed with him.

"Well, well! You must be Kismet!"

"Yes, sir."

"Where you from?"

"Up north, a couple of day's travel."

"What's the news from up there?"

"News, sir?"

"The caravans? See any in your wanderings?"

"No caravans. The people coming north are a steady trickle but I saw no large groups."

"That can't be," Kirk said. "The news is full of them, thousands at a time. It's on the news every night."

"They're pretty dispersed north of the city as far as I could see."

"You must have not been looking in the right places."

It was at that moment I realized Evelyn Rossi had married a rich idiot. No one took what the propapundits said at face value. Grammy made a sport out of hate-watching them and there was entertainment value in listening to my grandmother's commentary on the string of lies spewed. "Set a timer!" Grammy would crow. "Betcha they can't go one minute without spewing a lie I can spot in a snap."

Arthritis crept through her bones so she couldn't snap her fingers without pain anymore. She said "in a snap" in lieu of doing so.

"Wanda, I'm going to borrow Kismet for a few minutes. You haven't shown her to her room yet?"

"No, sir."

"C'mon. Got a nice surprise for you up there."

I put down the knife and ran water over my hands so I wouldn't smear beet juice everywhere. As I followed him, he pointed to a piano crammed into a corner off the dining room. "See that space? That's a nook. Other places in the house are called crannies. This house was one of the originals. Not many originals in New Atlanta. The city already burned down once and then a good portion of it was plowed under to make way for our retreat. I hardly live in this house but I'm mighty proud of it." His tone was friendly, but too familiar too soon.

After we climbed one set of stairs, Kirk was already panting and his face flushed red. "I have a minor heart issue," he explained. "Can't do too many stairs at a time but fortunately — "

I thought he was reaching for a door but it was a wide panel in the wall that concealed the entrance to a small elevator.

Kirk ushered me in first and then stepped in, slid the door closed and pushed a button for the fifth floor. He faced me and the quarters were so tight, I felt his quick breath on my forehead. "This is part of the house that isn't original. Added the elevator at the same time we put in the garage and our house next door."

The heat of his body radiated off him and I pressed my back in the wall.

"Evelyn tells me you're twenty." He touched his hair in a prissy way, as if I were a mirror and he was inspecting his reflection. "What do you think of Atlanta so far?"

"So far I've seen a dead man in a shelter, a prison break and a woman shot who was trying to help. Two CSS got hurt. I was nearly shot and then I was arrested. They didn't treat me very kindly, either."

I would have thought a normal reaction to my litany of the day's trauma would have set him back a step. Kirk Rossi was undeterred. "Quite an adventure for you."

Maybe they really are aliens, I thought.

"Anyone back home missing you?"

"My grandmother."

"Ah, yes. My wife mentioned that. But no brothers? Or boyfriends?"

I was relieved the elevator car lurched and squealed to a stop. When I made for the door he did not move at all so I had to squeeze past him.

Though the elevator stopped on the fifth floor, my room was actually in the attic. A ladder led up to a dark square in the ceiling. Kirk pointed the way and I climbed the ladder past a trap door. I was sure he was watching my behind closely.

So this is what it's going to be like. I'm not putting up with a lech. I won't be here long.

As I got to my feet, a low buzz preceded a weak light in the ceiling popping on. A large white dollhouse sat in a corner to my left among several cardboard boxes. A clothes closet on wheels and a chest of drawers stood on my right. My backpack lay on the narrow cot in the middle of the room. Someone had rifled through it and cast my belongings aside carelessly.

The sloped roof was low so when Kirk Rossi followed me up the ladder, he had to hunch to avoid banging his head. "Kind of grim, isn't it?"

"It'll do." A trickle of sweat ran down my neck. It had to be several degrees hotter in the attic than it had been in the kitchen with the stove on. A window stood in a gable at the far end of the attic. I went to the window hoping to catch a breath of cool wind but the air stood dead still.

Grammy would say, "The air may as well be a sweater." I missed her and wondered how she was feeling this evening. Standing in this strange room with this odd man behind the Select's walls, I guessed I would never see my grandmother again. It felt as if I'd taken a couple of days to get to Atlanta but the road back may as well have been across the stars.

"Wanda and Eye will keep you busy so I don't imagine you'll have much time to do anything here but sleep. We don't allow visitors so you'll have to find your entertainment within the family." He smirked. I didn't want to read further into what that remark might mean.

"Mr. Rossi, Wanda said you could arrange for a portion of my wages to get to my grandmother in Campbellford."

He seemed a little put-off but nodded. "I can arrange that. I have a bonus for you right away."

"Oh?" I didn't care for the way he looked at me. My gaze slid to a dusty freestanding lamp at the edge of the room. I wondered, should I need it, was the base hefty enough to do his skull damage?

And if it did, how're you going to escape the Circle alive, genius?

"Your predecessor left our employ in a hurry. Tanya was curvier than you but you may find something that will fit. Her clothes are where she left them, in the closet and the chiffonier."

Chiffonier? I decided he meant the dresser. Wanda was right. I was in high cotton.

"Why don't you try on a few things?"

He gave no indication he intended to move.

"I'll look later," I said, "when I'm alone."

"Suit yourself."

But I'd caught his annoyed look before he could cover it up with casual denial. I would have to watch him. I wondered if his wife knew about how he acted with girls in his employ. I didn't have to wonder long.

"Hello again, Kismet." Evelyn Rossi's head appeared at floor level. If not for the circumstances, the appearance of her disembodied head might have been comical. She must have crept up the ladder very stealthily in order to eavesdrop.

"Kirk? Don't you have some notes to go over before the evening meeting?"

He seemed smaller under her withering glare. "Yeah, yeah. I'll get right on that, peach." He turned back to me. "It's an old house and we treasure it. I just came up to say that we don't want any candles burning up here. You're probably used to using candles where you come from but we don't do that here. Fire hazard."

"I understand, sir. Like you said, Atlanta already burned down once."

Looking at him with his sheepish grin, sweating in the pale light, I had what Grammy would call a passing fancy. I thought it might be nice if Atlanta went up in smoke again, the part within the Circle's walls, anyway.

CHAPTER NINETEEN

Evelyn stood silently as her husband made his way down the ladder. She waited until we couldn't hear his footsteps on the wooden floors anymore. "Mr. Rossi is a flirt at times but he *will* take no for an answer. See that you always say no."

"Mrs. Rossi, this day started ... I don't know. It feels like this morning was days ago. I'm exhausted, I'm smelling funky and I did not give Mr. Rossi any sign that I — "

She waved her hand, silencing me. "Moving on, now that you're in my home, I need to make you aware of several ground rules. Wanda will educate you on the routines of this house and the chores for which you will be responsible. I need to speak to you about today."

"May I sit? I wasn't kidding about being exhausted."

"Please?" she prompted.

"May I sit, please?"

Reluctantly, she gestured for me to be seated. With great relief, I took my place on the cot. I could barely keep my eyes open.

"Several of the prisoners who escaped this morning have already been apprehended."

I wondered if Picasso was among them but even knowing his name might be considered too close an association. I remained silent and watched as she paced back and forth in the small space.

"Did you notice that there were no red jumpsuits among the prisoners this morning?"

"No, ma'am."

"Well, there weren't. Do you understand the significance of the color red within our justice system?"

"People who wear the red jumpsuit have been convicted of sex crimes. The Select chose red because some people are proud of what they do even when they shouldn't be. I've been present when a convict announces him or herself proudly. Perhaps they are too stupid to be ashamed. Maybe they listened to the wrong people and didn't understand that they weren't taking a stand. They were making a confession. When these people confess their crimes, they often speak of love. That's why we chose red for their jumpsuits. Red is the color of the heart so it is associated with love. Red is also the color of danger. Do you understand?"

I nodded.

"My husband has a soft heart. He asked for mercy for your predecessor and so she was merely ... "

Banished from the safety of the Circle forever, I thought.

"Fired," Evelyn said.

Her implication was clear. Kirk Rossi had flirted with Tanya Dunford. Maybe he forced himself on her or maybe, as his employee, she simply didn't think she could refuse. That amounted to the same thing. My mind reeled at the thought and again, I wished I had my knives.

"We have laborers who come inside our walls every day, tradesmen, mostly. Construction work needs to be done. We need some outsiders to maintain our way of life. You would do well to remember who you represent when you go about your business for the Rossi family. You are to be polite and quiet around the family and, to maintain security, circumspect around strangers. Do you know what circumspect means?"

"I do. You ask that I be discreet."

"So you have the words but do you know what it means in practice?"

"Don't tell anyone anything they don't need to know, I suppose."

"Anything else?"

"Don't get too friendly with the help even though I am the help?"

"I would have preferred you leave it at 'don't get too friendly with the help.' If you require companionship, Wanda will have to do."

I took this to mean that, in addition to avoiding her husband's advances, I should avoid any plumber who might enter her domain, also.

"Am I going to have any trouble with you, Kismet?"

"No, Mrs. Rossi. I'm just grateful for the opportunity. I slept on concrete last night."

Evelyn's smile was not a pretty thing. Something about the way it failed to reach her eyes suggested an underlying carelessness. I'd saved her child that morning but she had money. She didn't need me. I felt disposable. I was certain that no matter how long I might serve her, that feeling would not fade.

"Your predecessor took Eye outside the gate without permission. You are never to do that. Understood?"

"Yes, ma'am."

"The person who slept in that bed was a silly girl. She thought she knew what was best. She had no idea. That's the trouble with stupid people. They are so sure of themselves. I rose to the position I hold today because I was right, every step of the way. But I was righteous, too. Do you read the Bible, Kismet?"

"My grandmother read it to me when I was little." The words were a maze in which I could get lost. Bible readings helped me fall asleep when Campbellford nights got too hot.

"Psalm 34:17," Evelyn said. "'When the righteous cry for help, the Lord hears and delivers them from all their troubles.' I stand among the Select, delivered from all my troubles because I am righteous."

I couldn't help but think of all the Bible verses that spoke to the suffering of the poor and sick. I was almost moved to argue but this was neither the time nor the place. The truth was, all I wanted to do was eat, sleep and be left alone. Evelyn took my silence for agreement.

She gave me a long look and sighed as if a great burden had been lifted from her shoulders. "All that's left are the little things. If you have questions, always ask Wanda first. She's been with the Rossi family forever and has forgotten more than you'll ever know. The bathroom is downstairs. You will want a shower. It's early but, as you say, you are exhausted. Have a shower and I'll have Wanda leave your dinner at the top of your ladder."

I felt like a small, naughty child being sent to bed.

"Use the other girl's soap and shampoo." Evelyn gestured vaguely. "They must be here among her things somewhere. Do you know what a Navy shower is?"

"Turn on the tap so I get just enough water to get wet, lather, rinse off, conserve water."

"Correct. However, you will be happy to know that you may shower every other day." She smirked. "We can't have you running around with Eye smelling funky."

Evelyn slipped her hand into a hidden pocket of her dress and withdrew a gold key. "This key is yours. You will not lose it. I'll get Wanda to find you a necklace to put it on so there will be no excuses." Careful not to touch me, she dropped the key into my upraised palm.

She pointed to the trap door over the entrance to the attic. "It gets hot up here. You can leave the door open through the day and get some air in. At night, close it and lock it, for privacy. Very well?"

"Very well, ma'am."

In case her husband got any ideas, it was clearly my responsibility to keep him locked out.

"I have a key, too. You can be locked in, if necessary."

Though my eyelids felt as if there were heavy weights on them, a surge of anger roused me. "For security reasons?" I asked.

Evelyn's smile conveyed no warmth. Content to let me fill in my own answer, she began to climb back down the ladder. When she was nothing but a disembodied head again, she paused. "I can tell you're a clever girl. Never think you can be too clever with me. I wasn't always a Select. I know the secret thoughts of servants. I remember what it feels like to be part of the background, nothing more than furniture. Sometimes I even miss that feeling. You have no idea of the number and weight of all my responsibilities since I came to the position I have now."

"It must be a burden," I said.

"See? That's the sort of thing I mean." Evelyn mocked me in a high, childlike voice, "It must be a burden."

"Ma'am — "

"It could be earnest sympathy but we both know it's not. It's sarcasm. That won't serve you well or long in my house. You might fool someone born to the Select but I was not to the manor born. Even they let slip that they haven't forgotten I'm not one of them. I didn't go to Brandeis."

I didn't know what Brandeis was. My main concern was having enough food to eat, having enough money to send to Grammy and getting a good night's sleep. My highest aspirations were what the Select took as a given.

"You remind me a little of myself at your age, Kismet. There's something about your look that is inherently insolent."

"Grammy calls it 'resting bitch face.'"

Evelyn laughed. "Your grandmother is not wrong. If I see too much of that look, you could be out of here just as fast as your predecessor. From now on, unless you want to express heartfelt thanks to me, lower your eyes in my presence."

Like wolves, Picasso had said. *A direct look in the eyes is a challenge.*

I bowed my head. "Yes, ma'am."

"You might do, after some training."

"I really am glad I'm here and I do appreciate the opportunity. Thank you so much, Mrs. Rossi. You'll never know how grateful I am."

Her nod of approval gave me a genuine smile. Despite her certainty that she could read me, I could lie to her face convincingly.

CHAPTER TWENTY

I awoke back in Campbellford in my own bed. Judging by the angle of the sunlight slanting through the window, it was mid-afternoon. Disoriented, I sat up and looked around my small bedroom. Sissy and I had bunk beds when we were little but the top bunk got too hot so we scrounged twin beds, side-by-side.

Several pictures hung along the wall. Mostly there were photos of Sissy and me as babies. I was always the baby and so I was babied. She became a little jealous of that. At seven and five, she looked possessive of me, as if she were my protector. At twelve and ten, we are both sitting on a couch with a couple of feet between us. I'm smiling but, by the look on her face, Sissy was a little sick of me. In our early teens, we fought. I can't say when that stopped but by the time she left to join the Air Force, we were the best of friends.

Our only sticking point was that she didn't want me to call her Sissy anymore. "The whole world can know you as Susan Beatriz," I said. "Only I can call you Sissy."

"Once I get to Air Force School at Wright-Patterson, I can become a different person, reinvent myself."

"Why the change?"

"I'm not a kid anymore, Kismet. I'll be a full citizen soon and I want to be taken seriously," she said. "How do you suppose I'm going to get to be a flight surgeon if anyone calls me Sissy? Susan is my name. I'm not ashamed of it."

"You know what I think? I think you're trying to pass."

"Pass?"

I gestured toward her face and mine with circles. "You know what I mean. No matter where you go, you'll be a Susan. Don't forget where you came from. You really think going from Sissy to Susan will make much of a difference? It's not the name that will hold you back. It's the people in charge calling us Latinxiles — "

"You're just echoing Daddy."

"Is he wrong? He should be a lieutenant by now. He'll be a corporal forever. Anyone with a Spanish name taps out at corporal while every white boy from Texas is fast-tracked to eat in the officer's mess."

"If I come back on leave with a doctor on my arm, you better call me Susan then or I'll knuckle up and blast you right in the nose."

I agreed. The memory made me smile but something was wrong. The bunk beds were gone. So were the twin beds. Now there was only the narrow cot from the Rossi's attic. My gaze came to rest on the empty spot where my sister's bed used to be. I looked down at my body. I wore a filmy white gown that looked like my mother's wedding dress. I'd never worn anything so fancy.

Something was wrong. Sissy wanted to be a flight surgeon but that was not what was decided for her. The powers that be assessed her aptitude and chose another life for her. Instead of getting funneled into the Air Force's medical track, she was tasked to work in Intelligence.

Then I saw my dog, Quentin. Excited, he circled the garden, barking and wagging his tail, so happy to see me. I was happy to see him, too. Though his presence filled me with elation, I knew it couldn't be right. I looked to my father and sister for an explanation.

"Is this real?"

They said nothing.

"I'm dreaming, aren't I?"

When I looked back at Quentin, he was nothing but a pile of bones.

At that, the dream became lucid. I walked out of the bedroom and looked for Grammy but she wasn't in the house. I heard someone outside and went to the window.

Sissy and Daddy waited patiently in the backyard. We were supposed to call them victory gardens but everyone we knew referred to them as survival gardens. We grew tomatoes, carrots, beets, radishes, cabbages, and beans. The root vegetables seemed to fare best.

I didn't have to run to them. With a thought, I found myself standing beside them. My smile faded as tears slipped down my father's cheeks.

"When Louisiana and Florida flooded, I was glad to be deployed there to help," Daddy said. "When Vegas became a ghost town, I assisted with the evacuation. Same with helping to fight the Californian wildfires. Then they sent us to San Francisco. Guys from the South were surprised to find liberals owned lots of guns, too. While conservatives bragged about their weapons and posed with them in camo, liberals had been preparing, collecting arms quietly. The battle for San Jose turned into a hot mess."

"Where's Mama?" I asked.

My sister looked at me as if she wanted to say something but had been struck mute.

Daddy spoke for both of them. "The Army says your mother can finally come back but her leg won't come with her."

"I don't understand."

"If she stays in service, she gets to keep the prosthetic leg and her citizenship. Otherwise ...." He shrugged.

"But she lost her leg on duty! This isn't right!"

"Cutbacks. They cut care for veterans first."

"This isn't fair!"

"Oh, my sweet girl," Daddy said. "Haven't you learned yet that fairness has nothing to do with anything?"

"Where is she?" I asked again.

Sissy's eyes went wide. She seemed close to bursting.

"You can speak. Tell me."

My sister seemed relieved. "You don't know where Mama is so we can't know, either!"

I turned away. I could feel the tears on my cheeks and, for a fleeting moment, I was in two worlds. I stood with my father and sister in the dream, lucid and eager to fly away. But I was also locked in a sultry attic room in a narrow house within the Select's fortress. In the distance, from far beyond the horizon, I heard a chant that I could not quite make out. It had a cadence to it that, after a few moments, transformed into a march. Thousands of feet pounded concrete and chanted something ... something ...

I'm losing the dream, I thought. In a moment, I'll be awake. I'll lose them.

Again. I'll lose them again.

I turned to say goodbye to my father and sister but they were gone. Our little vegetable crop had disappeared, as well. All that was left was the burnt earth.

I awoke from the dream before I could fly away. Drenched in sweat and tangled in sheets, I struggled to extricate myself from the bed and staggered to the window. My breath came fast and my pulse pounded in my ears. Craning my neck, I gasped for fresh air but found no respite. At night, Atlanta was an oven.

The sound that had woven itself into my dream remained. That much was real. The chant and the thunder of many feet echoed among the city's buildings, alleys and canyons of glass and concrete. Off New Atlanta's walls, the motto of the Resistance rose in an angry, quickening war cry. "Don't hope. Do. Don't hope. Do! *Don't! Hope! Do!*"

Despite my distance from the nearest gate, the shouts seemed to arc over New Atlanta. Soon, the rise and fall of civil defense sirens competed with the march of the Resistance. I had no doubt which side would prevail. If Mama were here, she'd say, "The people with more firepower. That's the way to bet."

I heard gunfire.

I returned to my narrow cot, pulled the sheet over my head, squeezed my eyes tight, and covered my ears. It was not enough to block out the screams.

CHAPTER TWENTY-ONE

I awoke to someone tapping on the trapdoor. Gravity felt stronger than usual as I forced myself to sit up. Bleary and still tired after a fitful night's sleep, I called, "Who is it?"

"It's Eye!"

I hurried to unlock the trapdoor. When I looked down the ladder, I found my new charge standing in the hallway holding a bowl of oatmeal.

"I brought you breakfast," she said. "I told Wanda we should give you a welcome breakfast and she agreed as long as I got you up and going. She's worried you're lazy."

I rubbed the sleep from my eyes. "Thanks. C'mon up."

Balancing the bowl in one hand, she climbed the ladder. "Get any sleep?"

"Probably doesn't look like I did."

"The sirens kept me up for a while, too. Rebels tried to rush Gate 15 last night."

"Is that what happened? How do you know? Did they get through?"

"Mother gets all the news first." Eye seemed very proud of that fact. "Don't worry. They didn't get within a hundred feet of the gate before the parrots hit them with sound cannons. They were driven back."

I'd heard about such crowd control techniques from the propapundits. Sound cannons were supposed to be non-lethal means to pacify "riotous elements." However, not all the noise from the previous night was entirely benign. "I thought I heard gunshots."

The girl shrugged. "I've heard that lots of times. The sound cannons can't be everywhere. Mother says when that happens, it's the parrots firing over the heads of the crowd to scare them away."

Several refugees who'd run north through Campbellford told a different story. Not all the Select's strategies were non-lethal. The crowd control devices they used could blind or burst eardrums. I wondered how much truth Evelyn Rossi shared with her daughter.

"I want to thank you again for yesterday," Eye said. "Those men scared me."

"Me, too."

"But you came to the rescue."

I shrugged. "Had to. Whatever they had planned, it was going wrong. You stepped up for me, too. I think I was more scared of the CSS."

She waved that away. "The escaped prisoners were scary but the guards are there to protect us. They're our friends."

"Sure." I ate my oatmeal while Eye poked through Tanya Dunford's clothes to find something for me to wear.

Eye was a slight girl but moved with the confidence of someone older.

"Eye, did Tanya tell you why she took you outside the wall?"

"It started with a bad book," she said. "I didn't know it had been banned. If I did, I would have gotten in big trouble."

"What book?"

Eye tiptoed over to the trapdoor and checked to see if we could be overheard. Satisfied we were alone, she came back and whispered. "I never read it but Tanya had and she told me about it. I thought it was okay because she said it was about religion." Eye glanced over her shoulder nervously. "Tanya said that I was like the prince at the beginning of the story."

"I don't understand."

"There once was a prince whose mother, the queen, died. It was prophesied that the prince wouldn't just rule his kingdom. He'd rule the world. Thing is, after his wife died, the king kind of lost his mind with grief. He wanted to protect his son from all the bad things in the world so the king decreed that all the sick and old people had to leave the city. All the prince ever saw were young, happy and healthy people. Tanya said that the prince was looking for enlightenment so he could be a good ruler someday. To learn what life was really like, the prince had to go outside the castle walls. Tanya said that if I was going to take over for Mother when I come of age, I should see what it's like outside the Circle."

"I see. So your mom didn't know you were going out?"

The girl rolled her eyes. "Of course not. I thought it was going to be an adventure but we barely got outside the gate and I hardly saw anything. Tanya got fired for taking me. Wanda almost lost her job, too, but I told Mother and Father that Wanda didn't know."

That was interesting. "So Wanda did know?" I asked.

Her eyes went wide with surprise as she realized she'd said too much. I waved away her concerns. "Forget I asked. You don't have to tell me anything."

"Mother had a long talk with me about the city. She says she understands and that I will be able to go out someday, but not anytime soon."

"So you still want to see Atlanta?"

"Are you kidding? Just knowing you can't go anywhere makes the Circle feel like prison."

Eye's position within the Select Few would be the envy of anyone I'd ever known but curiosity is a powerful force. As much as I wanted to see how the Select lived, Eye wanted to go slumming.

"I'm surprised your mother is okay with you going outside the walls anytime in the future."

"Mother says that to understand how bad things are, I will have to see it with my own eyes. Tanya's mistake was not asking first. And we took Father's car. No wonder we got the prisoners' attention."

"What do you want to see when you go?"

"Oh, you know, how common people live, what they do, what it's like out there. The poor will always be with us but I wonder if that's true. If things are as bad as I hear, how will they keep living?"

I noticed how casually Eye had thrown out the edict that "the poor will always be with us." I wondered if she knew the full quote.

From what I remembered of my grandmother's reading of the Bible, Jesus scolded his disciple because he knew he would soon die. The gist was that Jesus was saying the apostle could concern himself with caring for the poor anytime but the Son of God didn't have much time left on Earth. I remembered the passage so well because I managed to annoy Grammy by debating her. "That sucks," I told my grandmother. "We're poor. There's no way out? I've got a better inter-pretation," I said. "Here's what Jesus should have said — "

"Kismet, don't test me or God," Grammy warned. "Don't be tellin' me what my Jesus shoulda said."

"He should have said the poor will always be with us, as in 'on our side.' When things go bad, the poor have to stick together. The Select Few have money. Our only power comes from looking out for each other, like when Mr. Dobbs broke his leg and we brought him food. The whole town looked out for him."

Dobbs had not repaid our kindness. Instead, he almost killed us all. Not all poor people stuck together.

"I have a bunch of friends who go to boarding school in Switzer-land," Eye said, seemingly out of nowhere. "They live like everyone here, but without walls. The Swiss banished all their poor. Those girls might never see anything interesting."

As if desperation was a museum exhibit to be looked at and then forgotten. I wasn't sure if it was freedom she craved so much as poverty tourism. I finished my cold oatmeal in silence.

But perhaps I wasn't so different. I was curious about the Select Few. I wanted to know how it felt to be free from fear. Inside the Circle, there were still plenty of dangers but the cot was better than concrete and I'd never starve. I could let Kirk and Evelyn Rossi worry about the money and all I had to do was take care of their child.

When I looked at Eye, a princess safe in her castle and destined to be a queen, I kept my thoughts to myself. I nodded at everything she said, agreeable and compliant. And for that, I began to hate myself a little more than usual.

I had to complete my mission before the full moon and I had no idea how to accomplish the feat. In the meantime, I would enjoy the benefits of living inside the Circle while Tanya was out there somewhere, probably sleeping on a hard floor and suffering from an empty stomach.

CHAPTER TWENTY-TWO

Eye was to take me on a tour of the neighborhood but first I had to complete several chores. Wanda handed me a red apron with white pinstripes and told me what to do. The kitchen dishes had to be washed and dried and the toilets needed to be scrubbed. Eye, Wanda and I lived in the narrow house. Evelyn and Kirk Rossi ate in the house but all their living and working was done elsewhere, places I was not yet authorized to go.

As I went about my work, Eye had her studies. I passed her several times through the morning. Her eyes were fixed on a screen and she wore headphones. Curious, I glanced over her shoulder. In the first hour, she studied Portuguese. The next time I looked, I heard her repeating phrases on the screen. I was pretty sure the soft sounds she made were Mandarin.

I was sweeping the kitchen floor around noon when Wanda offered me a protein shake. The taste was supposed to mimic chocolate, a flavor I only dimly remembered from early childhood. The glue-like mixture tasted more like brown chalk.

Eye appeared at the kitchen door. "I'm finished studying. Let's go!"

I looked to Wanda for permission but that was the wrong move. She sneered, "Go on, then. Don't look to me. You have your orders from the little one. Take the grand tour! Just be back in time to help me prepare dinner for the family. I'll show you how to make the polenta for when I'm dead."

I began to take the apron off but Wanda stopped me. "Whenever you're down here or go outside, we wear the apron."

I was about to protest because of the heat but thought better of it. After we were out of Wanda's earshot, I asked if she was sick.

"The 'for when I'm dead' thing?" Eye smiled. "Nah, she's not dying for anything except sympathy. Wanda's been talking like she's about to die any second for as long as I can remember. She says it's best to be prepared to die. Wanda doesn't like surprises."

We took a left out of the narrow house and my gaze fell on the houses next door. Two guards in blue uniforms and white gloves walked up the ramp to the big house on the far side. They paused at the front door and keyed in entry codes. The house was fairly unremarkable except for the heavy bars on the windows over steel shutters. Peering closer, I thought I saw what might have been gun ports.

"Best not to stare at the Security Center, Kismet," Eye whispered. "They have cameras."

I wheeled around. "Sorry, of course. Just ... everything's so new to me, that's all."

"I'll tell you a secret. A lot of people here own a bunch of buildings. There really aren't many Select Few. "

"The few aren't many," I said. "Makes sense."

"Well, I mean, especially since the massacre."

Heat rose in my cheeks and my breath caught in my throat. "Massacre?"

"Father says a bunch of the tech bros fled to their doomsday bunkers in Switzerland. Some went solo to compounds in Alaska. I'm talking about the sinking of the *Apollo's Lyre*."

Everyone knew about the *Lyre*. Several years previously, a massive cruise ship reserved for billionaires went down in a storm. Some people on Twitter could not contain their glee. It was rumored those indiscreet members of the Resistance were jailed.

Grammy told me that app used to be for everyone and was once helpful with organizing protest marches. After the sinking of *Apollo's*

Lyre, anyone could still join Twitter but only approved members with blue checkmarks were allowed to tweet. Some poor folks still managed to afford to watch the rich talk about their love of life and their fabulous lives. I couldn't guess why they would bother. We couldn't relate to them, only envy them. Every day, ordinary people were reminded of their ordinariness, spectators to a game we could never play.

Perhaps outsiders watched the rich at play in a sort of ritual of self-torture, flagellating themselves with treasures they will never possess. Maybe they told themselves they would, one day, be on the inside of that very exclusive club.

I did not share any of these thoughts with Eye. I was just the help and, by her mother's lights, my employment was tenuous.

"They said it was a tidal wave that took down the ship," Eye said. "That's not what people think around here. Mother thinks it was sabotage. *Apollo's Lyre* had a roller coaster on it! As Mother says, surely a boat with a roller coaster could handle some inclement weather. Father says it was a massacre, too, but it worked to our advantage. He says the sinking spurred funding for the Circle. Father had a piece of the contract for the construction of the wall."

Never let a good tragedy go to waste, I thought.

We passed the Rossi's other property on the near side of the narrow house. With its pink stucco, it reminded me of luxurious Spanish villas I'd seen in pictures. However, there were no windows on the first floor. I saw no doors. It was a pink stucco bunker. "Do you spend any time in your parents' house?"

"These three homes all belong to my father but I know what you mean. I go into the pink house on special occasions or when I'm invited to dinner. Wanda goes in more than I do, just to deliver food to their kitchen for Mother to reheat. She works a lot of long hours in the Security Center. She says it's just tidier if I stay with you and Wanda. When the time comes, Wanda will show you how to clean the hot tub and the pool out back. Tanya did that stuff."

"How long was Tanya here?"

"A few months, I think."

"You must miss her."

"Yeah, but Wanda says I shouldn't. Mother's pretty stressed about her."

"I'm sorry you lost your friend."

"Mother says we aren't supposed to be friends with commoners." Eye looked me up and down and I sensed she was wondering how much she should reveal. "We were friends, though," she added. "It's inevitable."

Her statement might have been obnoxious, but she was right. I laughed and so did she.

"Besides, if we were never supposed to be friends," I said, "how would your parents have ever gotten together?"

Eye put on a very arch English accent. "I want you to stick around so, please, never say anything about that. Mother does not appreciate being reminded of her humble origins."

"Okay, I can't take it anymore. What's with the British accent."

"It's the style," Eye said. "The Select are trying to get closer to their origins."

"I don't understand."

"Oh, you know." The girl waved my query away like a pesky gnat. "Things were simpler when we were colonizers."

I bit my lip. As we walked on I thought, *It's a good thing you're so cute, kid.*

Eye studied my face. "You remind me of Tanya, only better. She flouted the rules. You just don't know any better yet. Like Mother says, good training takes time."

I worried about the seeds that had already been planted in the girl's mind. There was so much she seemed to take for granted, ideas she accepted as known and carved in granite. Were I to stay in the Circle long, I wasn't sure I'd find her so adorable. I could befriend her as a child. If she became an adult who wrote others off as commoners, we couldn't be friends.

I accepted what my family told me, too. The seeds sown in me had been nourished well. My opinions about how people should treat one another were pretty much full-grown. For instance, Grammy would say, "Gratitude typically only lasts as long as it takes to express it. After that, it's screw you!"

I didn't blame Eye for accepting what she'd been taught. We all believe what we're told when we're young. Without more information, how could Eye end up any different from her mother? And who could resist becoming an entitled princess among American royalty?

Evelyn had grown up a commoner but ambition, perhaps love, had made her turn on her class. Why not? Who wouldn't change places with any member of the Select Few?

If the children were our future, we were doomed.

CHAPTER TWENTY-THREE

I walked with my charge through narrow, winding streets that looked like pictures from Old Europe. Every foot of space saved inside the Circle had saved the Select Few on their concrete wall budget.

"Do you miss those friends who went off to Switzerland?" I asked.

"Mother says it's better that I stay here. Getting an education abroad sounds good but things are going to get worse before they get better. If I'm going to lead someday, I should see things as they are. Too many people spend all their time getting mad about the past or are terrified of the future. That's what Mother says."

It was true that we spent a lot of time not being in the present. However, those who were mad about the past had plenty of good reasons to be angry. Anyone who wasn't terrified about the future counted themselves among the Select Few.

As if reading my mind, Eye added, "People call the people inside the Circle 'the Select.' Father says they call us that because they're jealous. He says there's a reason we are supposed to think of ourselves as the Select *Few*. There aren't many of us because, in any profession anywhere, there are the people who are at the top and then there's everyone else. Do you think that's true. Kismet?"

CHAPTER 23 • 129

This felt like dangerous territory. "Do I think what's true?"

"That we deserve to be here?"

"You're here so what does it matter what I think? Why do you ask?"

"I keep thinking about all those people who rioted last night. We have stuff they don't. I can understand why that would make them jealous, but sometimes I wonder if there's more to it. I've been jealous of other girls, but I never went outside their house at night to shout mean things."

Sensing my reluctance, the girl encouraged me. "You can tell me anything. I just want to know more about what it's like out there."

"Because you're the princess who lives in the castle."

"Stuck in the castle, yes."

"Eye, have you ever seen a dead body?"

"No."

"I saw one the first day I was here. I've seen quite a few bodies."

"What do their faces look like?"

"At the funeral parlor? Peaceful. The people who take care of that sort of thing make sure."

"And ... not at funerals?"

"The recently dead look drunk. One eye can go one way while the other wanders somewhere else."

She smiled. "Really?"

I nodded.

"How did you see recently dead people who looked drunk?"

"Refugees, on the road outside of my hometown. There was a purge when a big caravan came north."

"I didn't hear about that."

I shrugged. "I don't think anyone was supposed to know. It never showed up on a screen but I saw it with my own eyes."

As the silence stretched out between us, I became certain I'd been too honest. Eye felt the weight of this awkward pause. "Maybe I shouldn't ask too many questions," she said.

But at the mention of the dead, a need had already begun to grow within me. It felt like an ache over my heart, worse than a hunger pang. "Something's been bothering me. We should ... we should do something...."

I stopped and sat down abruptly. I couldn't seem to catch my breath.

"Kismet? Are you okay?"

I brought my head up from between my knees and managed a nod. "Gimme ... a minute. *T-t*-triggered *suh-suh*-something."

The night before, as the noise of screams and gunfire reached for me, I had retreated to my bed. I clamped my palms over my ears until I was sure the riot was over, immobilized by the noise rising above the wall. Still, the anguished cries of the mob grabbed at my heart. With each pulse, my chest felt tight, my breathing shallow and quick. As I squeezed my eyes shut, wishing the onslaught was over, I heard the distant rattle of machine guns.

At that moment, I wasn't in the Circle anymore. I was back on the outskirts of Campbellford not far from my home, hiding in the brush, barely daring to breathe, waiting.

Grammy told me not to go but curiosity claimed me. I was drawn by that same rattle of machine gunfire.

Machine ... gunfire.

It was almost as if the perpetrators themselves became machines: unfeeling, programmed, relentless and incapable of regret.

By the time I got there, the soldiers were leaving. Peering through thick branches, I glimpsed them. They wore the same uniform as my parents. From the woods, I heard one of them touch the muzzle and cry out as he burned his bare hand on the hot metal. The other soldiers laughed and crowed, "Noob!" as they climbed into a truck. They all carried backpacks, but these were not military-grade packs. I didn't understand that at first.

I waited, not sure it was safe to emerge from my hiding place. If they'd left a single scout behind, I would have been shot and left for dead like the rest.

Eventually, I crawled toward the road, alert for any sound. My breathing came harder and faster. The wind sighed through the tree branches above me. I waited a bit longer but I could detect no evidence of a living person besides my own pounding heart.

I got up into a crouch and rushed forward, keeping low, scanning the forest and the road frantically.

The people who'd been shot were not on the road as I had expected. The bodies lay in the ditch. Surprised and horrified, I tripped and fell, rolling in amongst them, on top of them. I gasped as I came face-to-face with a girl no older than me. Her eyes were blank, staring up into nothing.

There were hundreds of bodies in that ditch. The massacre stretched in both directions.

I'd begun to struggle to my feet when I heard a vehicle approaching. If I'd scrambled up out of that ditch at that moment, I surely would have been seen. I turned my head just in time to see a green Jeep coming around the bend at a snail's pace.

There was no choice. I went limp and lay with the dead. I couldn't see the occupants of the Jeep as they passed but I already knew what they were doing. In a moment, my fear was confirmed. A moan rose from someone to my left. A woman, I think, though pain can make any cry pitch to a higher register.

The Jeep stopped and the driver shut off the engine. I heard the crunch of boots on gravel.

"Make sure," someone ordered.

At a distance, machine guns rattle. Up close, the sound they make is more like an explosive bark.

The moaning stopped.

I listened for the crunch of gravel. The footsteps passed by slowly. The gunman must have been no more than a few feet away. I was almost sure he or she was just standing there, waiting for me to dare to open one eye, eager for me to panic and give myself away.

Eventually, I don't know how long, the soldier got back into the Jeep. The engine started up and they crept away to search for more survivors.

I wish it had ended there, but there was more. The mass killing of the refugees in the caravan made me ashamed that my parents wore the same uniform. But what did uniforms matter when the people giving orders had become ruthless?

Service and saving lives, I thought. *That's what it was supposed to be about. Not murdering unarmed civilians.*

I couldn't bring myself to feel much moral superiority, though. My parents always sent a portion of their pay home to Grammy and me. The money was late that month and there were rumors that military families wouldn't receive their payment until the next month.

The propapundits prattled on about cost savings and tight budgets. They didn't mention our empty stomachs. One blamed us for not having enough of a financial cushion against "hiccups in income." Another even told us to hold garage sales, as if we had anything left to sell, as if we had garages, as if anyone had any extra money to buy crap at a garage sale in the middle of winter.

We were living hand-to-mouth. That's why I couldn't just run home to Grammy. I stayed in that blood-soaked ditch and scrabbled through the pockets and the backpacks of the dead as long as I dared. I found food and jewelry. Afraid someone else would come along, I took what I could find of value and hid it in the woods. Then, weeping and disgusted with myself, I went back to gather more of whatever I could salvage.

To each victim, I whispered, over and over, "I'm sorry, I'm sorry, I'm sorry."

That still wasn't the worst of it. As I hid in the forest that day, going through my cache of treasures stolen from the dead, I heard voices on the road. At first, I thought the soldiers had returned. I was wrong. Others had heard the gunfire. I'd only been the first to investigate. I crept forward one last time to see people I recognized from town hurrying down the road. Through the woods, the townspeople came in droves. It seemed that most of Campellford came to bear witness to the carnage.

They weren't witnesses. A few stood in silence and turned away. Most scrambled down into the pit to crawl through the corpses, to find their own treasure. We were so desperate, we became a town of grave robbers.

We didn't see any government money for my parents' work for three months that winter. What I stole helped get us through. Not everybody made it. I heard of four suicides that Christmas, people who could not stomach what we had become.

I managed to sell some jewelry to keep Grammy and me alive. We ate the refugees' food. Knowing where those meals came from, every morsel tasted like ashes.

And still, that was not the worst of what came to be called the Campbellford Caravan Massacre. The worst came later, after the government checks began to arrive again. People from town didn't whisper about the cans of spam and dehydrated food rations anymore. We nodded to each other in the street. Each encounter was a silent message: You're a survivor. You're still here so you must be complicit.

The soldiers had done the deed and taken their finder's fee in loot. We were the vultures who swept in to pick the dead clean.

It was the lack of shame that got to me, trying to make the desecration into a virtue. By the time summer came and the crops began to poke out of the soil, people spoke aloud and easily of what happened to the caravan. Something elemental about Campbellford had changed. Our cruelty had become casual.

CHAPTER TWENTY-FOUR

M r. Dobbs, the sweet neighbor who'd once given me a ride on one of his ponies, said we should not be grateful to the people in the caravan.

"We should be proud to be strong, to do what it took to survive." He ate his beloved ponies so I guess he was true to his word.

"Our government is looking out for us," he said. "Those foreigners would have done the same. Financial realities being what they were, those soldiers did their duty and they saved us. Shot them and saved us. Saved the town!"

I fixed him with a hard stare. "You do remember there were little kids in that ditch, right?"

"Their parents shouldn't have brought them up this way."

"How bad would things have to be before you abandoned your home and walked to another country?" I asked. "Can you imagine how bad — "

Dobbs interrupted me, "It was us or them, Kismet! Would you rather be dead?" His tone hardened and grew louder. "You know how bad the harvest was, what with the drought we had! You comin' at me on your high horse, you're missing the simplest thing: To survive, we do what we must. There ain't enough for everybody."

"There would be if some weren't so greedy."

He waved me away. "Got a tragedy? It happens. Find what good you can and never let a good tragedy go to waste. Then, move on and get over it."

I noticed he was not debating right or wrong anymore. Staring into his face — so smug, so sure — my stomach folded and twisted in revulsion. "If things are that bad here, maybe we should have joined their caravan and went out looking for a better life."

My neighbor leaned on the fence and looked away to the horizon for a long time. For a second, I thought I'd gotten through to him. However, when he looked back at me, he said, "I'm sure it was hard for our troops — "

"I heard them laughing as they walked away!"

"In these situations, you have to make hard choices. Sometimes you have to think a certain way. Hating and laughing, it's all the same: a way to cope so you do what you must."

Dobbs spoke as if he were imparting wisdom as he twiddled with the crucifix that hung from his neck. I wondered if the crucifix was his or was it a remnant from his raid on the ditch?

"You learn all that in church, Mr. Dobbs?"

His face fell and he let out a tired sigh. "You don't understand war, Kismet."

"Funny you say that because I am in one. We all are."

Grammy said Dobbs talked that way to protect himself, to deny his self-loathing. I didn't care to hear any rationalizations. I began to hate Dobbs and so I was changed, too. I would never be grateful nor glad about what happened to the caravan.

That was two winters ago. The next winter, for a second time, the military pay stopped coming. Determined to avoid another massacre perpetrated on our behalf, the whole town worked together to ration our food.

Dobbs committed a crime against all of Campbellford then. I've told myself a million times since, I did what I had to do.

～

Listening to the familiar rattle of gunfire from Gate 15, I felt like I was creeping through the woods near Campbellford again.

The parrots in their perches would not show mercy. They would not fire over the heads of the demonstrators to warn them. Weapons are forged in fire. Through the heat of desperation, fear, greed or hatred, we had all become weapons.

Machine guns spit death. The soldiers in Campbellford were no different from the people atop the Circle's walls. They had all become machines. Before the Select Few rose to power, we had tools. We produced useful things. Now all our machines seemed to produce were fear and hate.

As I lay on my little cot in the attic of the narrow house and listened to the riot, the sounds were too familiar. I felt the gears of the State grinding people into pulp again. I tried to block out the visions of hundreds of dead. Still, their cries found me. Even high in the sultry attic deep within the safety of New Atlanta, the mob's shouts of anger and pain formed one voice that whispered through me.

"*Coward.*"

The dead in the ditch had whispered the same word. That's why, on his last leave at home, my father taught me about lucid dreaming in an attempt to banish the ghosts from my mind.

"I just want to be numb to it all, Daddy!"

"No, you don't. When you don't feel anything, you won't be you anymore."

"It hurts, though. In my heart and in my head, I swear it hurts like a real thing, something with sharp teeth and claws. Whatever it is, it's been with me since I fell into that ditch. It came back with me. In my dreams, I can almost see it. Each night, just before I *do* see it, I wake up screaming."

Daddy nodded. "I know what you're talking about. It comes in many forms, but I've seen that thing. I think it's the fear of what we could become."

"What is it?"

"You becoming something other than human, something worse."

"Like a machine," I said.

"You just have to sit with that fear a while. Give it time and you'll make sense of it. They say pain lets you know you're alive but that's a shitty way to look at it. I say, your fear means you still care."

"I don't want to care this much. I feel ... " I didn't want to admit what I felt but Daddy knew.

"Guilty. You feel guilty for being alive." He took me in his arms. "I'm glad you're alive."

"So what do I do?"

"Soldiers get PTSD, but civilians in war zones get it worse, lots of times. The drugs we take for it can be hard to find so the Army taught us about lucid dreaming. When the nightmares come, it gives us an escape hatch, somewhere to go to when that pain and fear won't let you alone."

"How does it help?"

Daddy smiled. "It's called lucid dreaming, not lucid nightmares. It helps you take control so nothing chases you when you're feeling helpless."

I had not mastered lucid dreaming. The nightmares still came sometimes. The corpses in the ditch sometimes rose from their mass grave — an open grave, easy pickings for vultures and unfeeling machines — and every face turned to me in silent condemnation.

I had survived at the expense of hundreds of innocents.

CHAPTER TWENTY-FIVE

"Kismet?"

"Huh? Yes, Eye?"

"You looked like you were a thousand miles away for a while!"

"Not quite that far ... never far enough."

"You muttered some things. You said we should do something."

"No, oh, yes!"

I had a question in my mind that needed an answer. In a way, I had a chance to go back to that ditch and maybe find a better way this time.

"Your mother doesn't want you going outside the wall. What if we were to go by Gate 15 and see what we can see? Safely, from this side?"

There is nothing so seductive as limits on what a child can and can't do. Going up to that barrier obviously appealed to her.

"I know a shortcut," Eye said. "Through my favorite place."

She waved for me to follow her and I did so on unsteady legs. We soon turned into a pedestrian shopping mall. The walls were glass and what I saw there made me gasp. It was as if I had stepped into a time machine. In every window, products I'd never seen in person were for sale.

Stern gray suits adorned mannequins, each with their plastic heads turned away. I imagined them looking off to a rich and hopeful future. Colorful, splashy dresses came next, but these were draped over real women. Each model was an impossibly tall Caucasian but with the epicanthic eye folds common to Asian women.

As I peered beyond the glass, handsome young men stood behind the counters at the stores selling women's fashion. It seemed that only beautiful young women worked in the stores selling men's clothes. I saw few customers.

"Eye? How do people make money?"

"What do you mean?"

"No one outside the wall has money to buy this stuff. Where does it all come from and how does anyone manage to buy it?"

Eye took a lot of things for granted, especially what she thought I should already know. "You know why I'm learning Chinese and Portuguese? Because China is where everything comes from. Dad makes most of his money out of his investments in Brazil. Why?"

"No reason," I said. "I'm made in America, that's all."

"That used to be a thing, didn't it?" Eye replied.

Perhaps to ease the tension, she broke out her best fancy British accent. "Mother says I should be grateful I don't have to study Hindi and Urdu. If India and Pakistan hadn't neutralized each other, I'd have to learn to speak the languages of their economies, too. I asked her, why not just use Google translate? She says that sets the bar too low."

"Speaking of setting the bar too low," I ventured, "I appreciate you showing me the city but I'm supposed to be helping you, too."

The girl looked skeptical. She said, "How can you help me?"

I heard: *How could someone like you help me?*

"Your mother mentioned working on vocabulary. Let me suggest more precision in language. India and Pakistan did not 'neutralize' each other. They shot nuclear missiles at each other."

"That did neutralize them, didn't it?"

"Nuclear strikes, tactical or not, is an issue close to my heart, Eye. The India-Pakistan war lasted a few minutes and killed about a billion people."

She leaned in conspiratorially. "We don't talk like that here." As if to explain everything, she added, "Foreigners are *foreign*."

"Oh."

She patted me on the shoulder. "If you want to fly under the radar here, you have to be more careful what you say and how you say it. As Mother says, not every thought needs to be spoken. Maybe we can go through a dictionary site, though."

I paused at a window and peered in at a glass case full of large men's watches. My father and mother both wore large Army watches on their wrists. The watch faces were large and the hands and compass were glow-in-the-dark phosphorous. Each had a strap to cover the glow so their positions would not be given away while they went on night missions.

I wondered what my parents would say if they could see these timepieces, each one a work of art in gold and silver with diamond accents. These watches were never meant to be worn by someone who walked with a rifle or cleaned a toilet.

Behind me, two men in gray business suits met in the mall's corridor. Their shoulders were so padded, I wondered if they could turn their heads and look to the side comfortably.

"A man of means among the blessed!" the first exclaimed in a plummy accent.

The second replied, "A person of substance among the blessed!"

I was to learn that was a standard greeting among the upper class, at least within the Circle.

Someone knocked on the glass from inside the store. Startled, I looked up to see a woman in a red striped apron wagging her finger at me.

"We should go, Kismet. They know you aren't here to shop."

I turned away, angry. I was only looking. What harm had I done? I hadn't even stepped inside their store. And to be scolded by another servant who wore the same damned apron? I shifted quickly from hot embarrassment to cold anger.

As Eye led me through the plaza and around a corner, I gasped. Two guards in deep blue uniforms wearing white gloves stood at the entrance to a grocery store unlike any I'd ever seen or imagined. Aisle after aisle of fully stocked shelves sat beyond polished glass. Leaves of various kinds of greens, bright orange and yellow peppers and apples were on display, not even in a vault. Brightly colored boxes and bottles sat on the shelves, just waiting to be scooped up without a thought to rationing.

Most staggering, there was no line and all the customers in the store took so much they needed big wire carts, not little baskets or hemp bags. The shoppers literally took more than they could carry! The sight brought me close to tears. Grammy had told me about such things. I wished she were here to share the sight.

Eye took my hand and pulled. "C'mon! I have to show you the best place in the whole Circle!"

"That wasn't it?"

"*This* way."

We came to revolving doors that opened to a tunnel that led to a staircase. As soon as we stepped through, my ears popped. The air was moist and warm. I smelled greenery.

At the top of the stairs, we were surrounded by trees, bushes and flowers. I looked around, bewildered at the tall oaks, ash and fir.

Eye stepped under a maple tree and watched for my reaction. "Well?"

"It's a little like being home."

"Is it, really? Wanda said you were a lamb from a farm."

"Not really a farm but surrounded by woods."

She seemed disappointed. "Sometimes the trees die in here but they replace them right away so it always looks good."

Probably pulled out by the roots and transplanted whole from the woods I'd traveled through to get here, I thought.

"You don't like it? At Christmas, we got a couple of chestnuts from a tree over there." She pointed. "We roasted them over an open fire, like in the Christmas carol. It didn't really taste very good but it was fun to do."

As with the grocery store, Eye and I saw different things. To her, this oasis of nature within New Atlanta was a pleasant nature walk. I'd seen plenty of trees in my life. The Select's arboretum would have been better used as a greenhouse to produce food.

"Is there a section for ... I don't know. Tomatoes?"

"We've got greenhouses and rooftop gardens all over the city and up along the railroad tracks," Eye declared. "But this is the best."

As I took in the girl's enthusiasm, it occurred to me that I was acting like what Grammy would describe as "a bit of a pill."

Eye stared at me expectantly.

"It's very nice," I said. "Shall we explore the path?"

"The arboretum winds around a bit under the helipads. After that, it'll take us straight to Gate 15."

And so it did.

When we got there, I put my hands over the girl's eyes.

Too late.

CHAPTER TWENTY-SIX

Gate 15 was a high and wide archway designed to allow the passage of big transport trucks. From the top of the stairs at the exit of the arboretum, we had a clear view of the street beyond the wall. A solitary CSS guard stood on the far side with a garden hose. The water pressure was insufficient to wash all the blood into the gutter.

Bodies lay in the street. Two more were still slumped against the bars of the closed gate.

Eye and I froze for a moment. The presence of bodies surprised her. It was not the sight of death that shocked me. It was the arrangement of the corpses that made me gasp.

The protesters had been shot where they lay in the street. They used their bodies, their deaths, as a message to the Select. The corpses spelled out: *EAT THE RICH*.

The emaciated girl who formed the bridge between the pillars of the H was probably no older than Eye. I guessed she'd died between her parents, her head cradled against her mother's breast, her father dead at her feet.

I covered the girl's eyes and led her back the way we'd come. "I'm sorry. You shouldn't have seen that."

Eye was quiet for some time. We dawdled amongst the arboretum's trees. Eventually, she spoke. "Why would they do that? That doesn't solve anything."

"I guess they were trying to shock someone's conscience."

"But even if they did, it won't help them! *They're* beyond help! They're dead! That was stupid."

I watched her for a moment and decided to hold my tongue. How could I explain sacrifice to someone who'd never experienced loss? How could I describe desperation to someone who'd never had a single pang of hunger? I may as well have explained magenta to someone blind since birth. Perhaps I should have tried, anyway, but the sight had me shaken up, too.

With each of us weighed down by our thoughts, it was a long and quiet walk back to the narrow house. I hadn't expected the protesters to make such a stark demonstration of their sorrow, their rage and their need.

Eye went to her room and I busied myself with trying to appear useful. As I was about to help Wanda prepare dinner, Kirk and Evelyn called me into the small office off the dining room.

He slouched behind the desk, disheveled in a wrinkled linen shirt. Evelyn stood against the barred front window, her arms crossed. In her dark blue uniform and bright white belt, shoulder strap and holster for her sidearm, she looked particularly severe. When she told me to sit in the chair opposite her husband, I felt like I was being ordered to take the witness stand. However, they had few questions. This was to be a monologue.

"On my first day of officer training school," Evelyn began, "each cadet was given a sheet of paper with a long list of instructions. Our instructor told us to read the whole sheet before we began. The first line asked you to write your name. The second was your serial number. After that, it was an odd bunch of requests. I don't remember all the details now. Things like drawing a triangle and shouting your name to the rest of the unit. It wasn't long before the first cadet shouted his name. I was a slow reader and feared that I would be left behind, that I would look foolish. Still, as ordered, I read the whole sheet of paper before I began to follow all the instructions."

Kirk interrupted his wife. "Eve, darling, is this really necessary?"

She winced as she touched her forehead. "Kirk, you know this is a strain for me. Just let me get through it."

Scolded, his gaze wandered to the ornate tin ceiling.

She continued, "I read the whole sheet, or thought I had. I would say I read to the bottom but didn't really process what I was reading. I didn't understand why a couple of cadets snickered as I got up out of my chair, stood at attention and shouted my name. It was only at the end of the exercise that the instructor began screaming at us. The last line on the sheet told us to fill out items one and two and ignore the rest. I was embarrassed, of course. I swear I read it but I was in such a hurry, it just didn't stick, do you understand?"

I nodded.

"I can't hear you!"

"Yes, ma'am. I understand."

"I doubt you do. You see, what I was supposed to take from that exercise was a lesson in listening carefully to orders and following them to the letter. That's not what I really learned, though. What I took away from that moment was I was not to trust anyone, not even my instructors. From that moment, it has always been difficult for me to trust anyone."

Kirk cleared his throat. "This is my wife's roundabout way of asking why you took Eye to Gate 15 this afternoon."

"Eye loves the arboretum. She took me on a tour of some of the Circle today, just to familiarize me with where everything is. When we came out of the arboretum, we were at the far end and, well, we saw —
"

"We know," Kirk said. "It is not general knowledge what happened at Gate 15 last night and we would prefer it to stay that way. People are already on edge."

"I feel a headache coming on," Evelyn said in her arch British accent.

I'd been amused by her pretense at first. I was beginning to hate it.

"You've added to my headaches, Kismet. I wanted to introduce Eye to the complexities rather more slowly."

Complexities, I thought. *That is a great euphemism.*

Kirk rose and put a hand on his wife's shoulder but he spoke directly to me. "It's the Circle versus the world. Every day, goods we need come to us by rail and the AUTONAVs. We are engaged in trade with various countries and regions. Several of those trade partners are, like us, surrounded by war zones. The Atlanta you lived in yesterday is a foreign country. Old Atlanta is an obstacle to the Circle sustaining itself, a barrier to our way of life. You're new here. Don't you like it? Isn't it better than whatever you came from?"

I nodded, careful to defer meekly, my gaze on the floor at their feet.

"I'm not sure this arrangement is going to work out," Evelyn said.

"I don't know what Eye told you, but we didn't try to leave the Circle or anything — "

"Eye didn't say anything about you. She didn't say anything about what she saw outside Gate 15 but when I found her in her room crying, I checked her tracker and the surveillance cameras. I had a suspicion and it panned out immediately."

Despite her complaints, Evelyn's smile betrayed her glee. She was pleased with herself for her quick sleuthing. The surveillance feeds were all routed to the house next door. She probably figured out where we went and what we saw in the span of a few minutes.

"I saw you with my daughter," Evelyn said.

"Well, that is what Kismet already admitted to," Kirk said. "And she did get her out of there quickly."

The look Evelyn gave her husband might as well have been the slash of a knife. He sat back down and went back to examining the ceiling.

I don't know whether she would have banished me back to what they considered a war zone. I didn't find out because Eye let out a scream from upstairs.

Evelyn and Kirk rushed for the door and I followed. They hadn't fired me yet and I was genuinely concerned for Eye.

At the top of the stairs, Kirk was flushed and panting. Evelyn got to her daughter first. She sat on her bed with one leg extended. She pointed, high up on her thigh. "It's a spider!" she cried. "And it won't come off!"

Evelyn cursed. Kirk stood panting in the bedroom door. I looked at the insect and recognized it for what it was immediately. "It's not a spider, honey. It's a tick."

Evelyn cursed again. "My expertise is urban warfare. I haven't had to deal with this. Kirk, call the doctor."

Eye moved to pull on the body of the tiny invader but I stayed her hand. "Don't yank on it. It looks like it's embedded fairly well. You don't want to try to pull it out or you'll leave the head under the skin."

"You've seen this before?" Evelyn asked.

"A dozen times, at least," I said. "There's a couple of ways of dealing with it. One is with lotion and the other is with heat. If I can have a candle, a match, a jar and a needle, we'll get that little thing right out."

Still pink and puffing, Kirk staggered to the stairs and bellowed for Wanda to bring the items.

A few minutes later, I heated the end of the needle. Evelyn stood back, her hand to her forehead, obviously in some pain but watching me carefully.

"Ticks are kind of like bed bugs," I told Eye. "You can hit 'em with a hammer and they don't much mind. My grandmother says the only virtue the little things possess is persistence in the face of adversity. To get this little nasty to pull his head out, you have to encourage him gently with a little heat on the rear end. We're just going to give this bug's butt a light spanking."

Eye smiled bravely as I applied the heated needle. The tick wriggled and began to pull out from sucking her blood. I tipped the insect into the glass jar and held it up for all to see. "There you are. All we need to do is clean the wound a little and your doctor can get this checked out."

The girl's eyes went wide. "It's out. Why do I need to see the doctor?"

Evelyn looked worried but it was Kirk who blurted his fear. "We don't want you to get Lyme disease, honey!"

"Lyme disease?" Eye echoed.

Evelyn looked cross with her husband as tears began to well in their daughter's eyes.

"The doctor can check it out, but Lyme is unlikely," I said, trying to sound confident for the girl's benefit. "You get more ticks like this when the deer population is high so I'm surprised it made it into the arboretum. It's the red ticks that are the worst. This is *not* a red tick." I shook the jar and the insect rattled a little. "They're nasty little vampires but you won't turn into Dracula. And even if you did, the doctor has drugs for that, I'm sure, right, Mrs. Rossi?"

She nodded. When she spoke, all pretense drained from her and the soft Georgian accent came through. "Don't worry, sugar. We've got something for that if worse comes to worst."

"But it probably won't," I added. "Why don't you go wash that leg and we'll find something to put on it, okay?"

Eye stood and, to my surprise, gave me a fierce hug. "Thanks, Kismet."

When she was gone, Evelyn cursed again. "It's that damn arboretum. She'd go there every day if we let her!"

"She'll be okay," I said. "Dozens of ticks, no Lyme disease so far. I've got a long winning streak with ticks. Used to pull ticks and porcupine quills out of dogs all the time."

Kirk laughed. "We didn't know we were hiring a vet."

Evelyn gave a grudging smile.

"Out in the Georgian woods, it's a common thing. I picked up a lot from my sister and grandmother. No hospitals around Campbellford but we deal with small things in country ways."

"Oh, really? Any country medicine for a throbbing headache?" Evelyn asked.

She was being sarcastic but I pretended the question was serious. "Wanda mentioned that you need a lot of quiet and to sit in a dark room sometimes. We had a neighbor down the road, Lisa Gott. She got migraines like that sometimes. If you catch it early enough, you can often shut it down before it gets going."

Evelyn looked up, suddenly interested. "How's that?"

"Plunge your arms into cold water. We didn't have ice but Lisa used to have a stream out back of her place. When you feel the migraine coming, shove your arms into cold water. Sissy says it's something about rerouting the blood so you don't get too much in your head when blood vessels dilate. Worked for Lisa. Maybe it'll work for you."

Evelyn nodded. "Thank you, Kismet. It may already be too late but I'll try that right now." She strode out of the room.

Kirk stood awkwardly in the doorway. I handed him the jar. "Better have the doctor take a look at that to see if Eye will need any more treatment. Maybe the doctor should see her, too, I don't know."

"To confirm your diagnosis?"

"Sure," I said.

"Evelyn told me about Campbellford," Kirk said. "I'm surprised you had any dogs. I thought they all got eaten."

"Used to have a lot of dogs around town. Then we had a couple of bad harvests followed by hard winter. We went through two famines."

He whispered to be sure no one else would hear. "The caravan massacre didn't get you through?"

"I didn't know many people knew about the massacre outside of Campbellford. It wasn't reported — "

"You think that tragedy only happened in your little town?" He gave a smile that reminded me of his wife. "Evelyn tells me things. With her work, we find out a lot of things regular people aren't supposed to know."

He seemed very pleased with himself. I liked him even less.

"The massacre got us through the first famine. It was the next winter when there were a lot fewer dogs in town. We worked together to try to survive, pooled our resources."

"That must have been hard," he said lightly, perhaps deceptively so.

"The day after Valentine's Day we discovered that someone had pilfered our supplies. Until we could find the missing food, we had to take emergency measures. That's when the dogs got eaten. We didn't want to kill our own pets so we traded."

"Oh, God!"

"That bought us another couple of days."

"Two days made a difference?"

"There was a trail in the snow from where we stored the communal rations. That petered out in the woods, but it gave a direction. Some enterprising young person from town suspected a relative of the guy who was supposed to guard the stores that night. It was a nearby farmer."

"Someone you knew?"

"Quite well. I had my suspicions so I confronted him first."

"*You* were the enterprising young detective?"

"When I accused him of stealing from the town's rations, he laughed and tried to bargain with me. He even asked for a kiss. 'A Valentine's treat,' he called it. Then he offered to share the food with me and my grandmother. He told me he'd be my sugar daddy and I'd be his sugar baby."

"What did the town do about the guard and the farmer?"

"Execution by hanging that same night."

Kirk's eyebrows shot high. "Quick country justice?"

"He was a neighbor I'd known all my life. His name was Clayton Dobbs."

"How do you feel about his death now?"

"My dog's name was Quentin. He was a cocker spaniel. I can't imagine he had much meat on his bones but it was an emergency situation. When peril pays a visit, anything goes to keep it out of your house. Dobbs himself once told me that. I loved Quentin much more than I cared for that farmer. My only regret is that I got to Mr. Dobbs and the stolen rations too late to save my dog."

"So you saved the town but it must have come at a high cost to you."

"I don't regret it. Dobbs had a huge old oak tree in his backyard. You could still see the tree house he'd built in that tree from when he was a kid. Still had a rope ladder and a tire swing. We used the rope from the swing to hang him and his co-conspirator. Same tree, too."

"God!"

I fixed Kirk with a piercing stare. "I would have hanged him just for asking for his Valentine's treat."

Kirk had been flushed before, his cheeks pink. When I left to see to Eye, he looked a little pale.

I doubted I had to worry about locking the door to my room after that.

CHAPTER TWENTY-SEVEN

For the next week, we stayed inside the narrow house. It was determined that the tick did not carry Lyme disease. However, Eye was still shaken at what she'd witnessed at Gate 15. I wasn't sure if we were ordered to remain indoors as a punishment or to give the girl time to recover.

Staying inside didn't really matter. The weather had turned ugly. Each night I went to my window to check the phase of the moon. Black clouds roiled over the city, issuing a near-constant downpour.

In addition to my duties assisting Wanda, I skipped rope with Eye in the underground garage. She knew songs to sing as we skipped that I'd never heard before.

The door to the Security Center stood a few feet away. I tried to get a sense of when the shift changes happened but the AWE guard's on-duty hours seemed staggered. Most of them came and went through the front door. I only saw Evelyn enter through the door in the garage and she always kept her key card on her belt.

When Eye grew tired of playing in the garage, we worked on expanding her vocabulary. A dry reading of the dictionary did not capture the girl's attention. However, when I made it a competitive exercise with a game of Scrabble, she was willing to play for an hour or two at a time.

Kirk called these sessions with his daughter English lessons. "It's a pity you aren't British. If you could mimic the accent, you'd be perfect."

"Perhaps you could hire a dialogue coach for Eye," I suggested.

"We had a maid from Trinidad when I was a boy. Wonderful accent! She went back to Trinidad. She should have stayed here. I suppose she's underwater now."

I couldn't manage a proper English accent. I couldn't really understand why the Select Few were anglophiles, either. The sun had long since set on that empire.

Kirk explained, "When a lot of people, especially Yankees, hear the Southern accent, they automatically deduct forty IQ points from the speaker. I went to a meeting to purchase a shipyard up in Halifax. I could buy and sell everyone in that conference room twenty times over. When I spoke, I had the feeling they wanted to check under the table to see if I was wearing shoes."

Eye watched videos to learn how to sound like a proper English noble from a previous century. I still thought it was silly but Evelyn valued those lessons on par with knowing not to drink from the finger bowl.

As torrential rain poured, Eye and I curled up on the couch in her room as if we were sisters. That afternoon, we played Boggle and worked on crossword puzzles together. We looked up words we didn't know and Eye repeated each word several times, perfecting her adopted accent.

Evelyn appeared in the doorway wearing a bathrobe. I'd sensed she'd been in the hallway listening.

Eye chuckled as she played with the British pronunciation of *aluminum*. She drew out the vowels. "Aluminium. *A-loo-min-ee-um! Aa-looooo-min-eeee-um!*"

"Well, aren't you two cozy! Eye, why don't you take a break from giggling with Kismet and work on your languages. If you think an English accent is difficult, try conjugating some Portuguese verbs, hm?"

Reluctantly, Eye left to get to work as I put the Boggle pieces away.

"She enjoys you."

"I enjoy her company, too."

"You know, I tried your trick to get rid of the migraines."

"Oh? And?"

"Didn't work, not the first time. However, I looked into it and the next time I felt the pain coming on, I did as you suggested right away. No headache! Thank you for that. Wanda says you're useful, too."

"I'm surprised to hear that. I never feel like I can do anything right when we're in the kitchen. Or if I do, it's not fast enough."

"Wanda may be crusty but she knows what she's doing. You'll learn a lot from her. If you don't learn how to make her polenta before she dies, Kirk will fire you."

"I'll do my best."

"I'm sure you will. Wanda is getting old and arthritic. I think you should cover some of her more physical duties. She'll give you an access card and show you all that's required to clean our house next door. Think you can handle this new level of trust and responsibility?"

I nodded. "Yes, ma'am."

She lingered at the door and asked, "Have you gotten over the culture shock of being inside New Atlanta yet?"

"I'm not sure what you mean."

"There's a big difference between living out there and living here. I have tried to protect Eye from certain realities, perhaps too long. After what she saw at Gate 15, she came to me bawling one night, worried that the commoners were going to break through and actually eat her. Can you imagine?"

I could imagine that, actually. Like many thoughts, I kept it to myself.

"Eat the rich. *Hmph*! And then what? Mob rule? Every flock needs a shepherd and that is the Select Few. These insurrectionists say we're only throwing them crumbs but at least they're getting that much."

That little.

"Somewhere along the way, people lost their ambition. They don't have what it takes to be of value or service and expect to be catered to. They contribute nothing so they are nothing. Bunch of malcontents and childish nihilists, they are!"

Nothing childish about nihilism, I thought. I'd played dead in a ditch and stolen from corpses. I knew despair. Those who have never known a crisis could not understand the impulse to give up on hope.

Evelyn put herself at the top. Having found herself at a great height, she was eager to break the ladder before anyone could come up behind her.

"The trouble with commoners is," Evelyn went on in her fake English accent, "they don't understand us or how the world works. It's much harder being among the Select Few than they can ever imagine. There are forces out there who would bring our wall down if they could. Given half a chance, they'd stage a repeat of the French Revolution, complete with guillotines. Did you know that Marie Antoinette never actually said 'Let them eat cake?'"

"I was not aware of that."

"It was propaganda put out by those who would destroy the upper class. Hundreds of years may pass but nothing's changed. It's just rumors and lies disseminated by seditionists bent on dividing us."

Dividing us? I thought. *You're the ones with the big wall!*

"We shoulder the burden of *noblesse oblige* and no one's grateful."

I sat there, listening to Evelyn rant and picturing hundreds of dead people in a ditch.

"The president and his sycophants catered to the ordinary people's whims. Our nation became a tinderbox. The politicians ruined everything. The Select had to step in. A beneficent dictatorship became necessary."

Beneficence? Is that what we had?

She shrugged. "No matter. As it is told in Corinthians, 'Even if our gospel be veiled, it is only veiled to those who are perishing.'"

Listening to Evelyn's rationalization of how the corporatists killed democracy, I was reminded of my mother cursing the Select Few.

"They're bringing the militia groups into the military!" Mama exclaimed. "Can you believe this? Well-regulated, my ass! These are the same fools who had a hand in blowing me up! I guess they finally found a way to make being in a bohunk militia pay."

"So I gather you don't approve?"

"I'm not joking, Kismet. Cops used to be called peace officers. We militarized them and now the CSS act like an occupying force in enemy territory. The Select call them centurions — not what *centurion* used to mean, by the way. Now we have as much war at home as we did in the Sandbox."

Mama and I were still in Bermuda then. I wish we'd stayed there. My mother was bitter, but she was safe.

She sat staring at the prosthesis where her leg used to be. "Love or hate us, it's all the same. The people who put us on a pedestal and the ones who spit on the uniform both think we're a monolith. I've served with geniuses and idiots, racists, sexists, heroes and cowards. Civvies don't see us as people. To them, we're either weapons or tools. As soon as we're no longer useful, we're as forgotten as a broken toy."

She didn't know then that the army would call her back into service despite her injury. That's the irony. She wasn't a broken toy. She was a lemon that had been juiced. The powers that be were determined to squeeze just a little more out of her. If she didn't comply, she'd lose her citizenship and the prosthesis along with it.

"Once upon a time," Mama told me, "people believed most other folks were good people. When we started to distrust each other, that's when the rot began to set in. We couldn't trust politicians and we didn't trust each other. Later, one in six people thought the military should take over the government. The elite rejected that but overcorrected. Corporations are running and ruining everything. Your generation calls it the Slow Apocalypse. It's not some grand conspiracy. Nobody's smart enough to engineer that. I'll tell you what it is. It's the law of unintended consequences come a callin'."

I dared to look Evelyn directly in the eyes for a moment. She smiled as she met my gaze. When she spoke about the inferiority of the poor and embraced her prosperity gospel, she believed every word she spoke. The rationalizations we give ourselves to escape the consequences of sin are powerful. She wasn't an evil mastermind controlling the gears that turned the world. Evelyn was an unintended consequence.

Me, too, I thought.

CHAPTER TWENTY-EIGHT

I sat at a picnic table in the arboretum, halfway between Gates 12 and 13. The clouds had broken and shafts of sunlight slipped through the trees. I wondered where my sister was and what she was doing. I supposed I could never know the details of all her duties. I was running out of time to get into AWE's Security Center and I had yet to find a way in. Time was running out.

An old man wearing the brown apron of a workman sat down at the table across from me. His large brown mustache reminded me of pictures I'd seen of walruses.

I said hello but he did not reply. He only stared at me as if he was attempting to guess my weight.

"Is there something wrong?"

"Fallen in love with luxury, have you?" he asked.

"I don't know what you mean."

"Why aren't you at work?"

"Sunday is my day off."

"Like it at the Rossis' place, do you? A cook, three meals, a nice place to sleep, the easy life?"

"I don't know who you think I am but you obviously don't know me. My life isn't easy."

He looked up, through the glass at the sky. "Can't quite see the moon from here. How long, do you suppose, before the full moon is upon us again?"

"Not long."

"Lotta people watching for that full moon. The folks in the refugee camp just south of the Circle are hoping to get better shelter. It's not time yet but I thought I should check in on you to see how you're doing."

"You don't know me and I don't know you."

"I know, I know. Army brat. You traveled around a lot. Spent some time at a rehab hospital in Bermuda looking after your mother. You're Kismet. Your sister's name is Susan but you call her Sissy. You've called her Sissy since you were little and she used to call you Kissy."

"How do you know all that?"

"You know how. That which is already known need not be spoken."

"I'm doing what I can."

"Are you? We know people. People are watching, folks you know nothing about."

"What do you want, mister?"

"Assurance that the little people have not been forgotten."

At that, rough hands grabbed my apron from behind and hauled back so hard I began to choke as the cloth cut into my neck. I couldn't see my attacker's face. All I could see was that he, too, wore a laborer's apron. From a sitting position, I wasn't prepared to defend myself. I kicked and struggled as the air left me and the coarse fabric of my apron burned my throat. I reached up and behind me and jabbed with my thumb.

The first time, I hit him in the nose. No effect. However, my failed attempt helped me navigate for the next strike. This time, I poked my thumb in his eye. I twisted as his grip loosened. As I began to stand, the first man struck me across the face with something hard and I fell to the ground, coughing and gasping.

Dazed, I began to stand and a younger man, holding a hand to his eye, placed his boot on my chest. He pinned me. The older man bent over and I watched his lips form a few parting words beneath his walrus mustache. "Don't forget why you're there. Full moon's comin' fast."

As I struggled to my feet, I was surprised to glimpse an AWE officer standing by the nearest exit to the street below. She stood frozen as my attackers ran past her. She stared at me for a moment before turning to leave in the same direction as the two men. Then she locked the exit door behind her so I would have no hope of following any of them.

Angry and confused, I wandered back to the narrow house, holding my left cheek the whole way. It felt like half my face was about to fall off. The Rossis' house would never feel like a home to me but I was glad to retreat there.

Kirk was on his way out when he met me at the front door. As soon as he saw me, his face fell. "What happened?"

There was no point lying. "I was attacked."

"Come into the office and sit down. I'll get you a towel and some ice."

The skin was not broken, just a bruise along the cheekbone and some swelling. Kirk was surprisingly tender as he applied a cold face-cloth to my wound. I ran my tongue over my teeth. None felt loose.

"Shall I call the doctor?"

I declined his offer. "Thanks, but it's more hurt pride than pain."

"Did they ... take anything? Touch you?"

"No, nothing like that. Just bullies is all."

"As soon as Mrs. Rossi gets back from church, I'll get her to pull the surveillance recordings. We'll find whoever did this."

"I have a strong feeling that any cams in the area were disabled."

"How could that be?"

Once again, I'd said too much to bother lying to him. "An AWE officer saw the whole thing. She didn't move a muscle to help and she locked an exit door behind the guys who did this."

"How could this happen inside the Circle? And why?"

I just shrugged.

Kirk steadied himself as he walked behind his desk and it struck me again how frail he was. He plopped down in his plush leather chair heavily and stared at me with a look I could not decipher.

"I should go," I said.

"No, stay a few minutes and keep the cold on your cheek. I am genuinely worried about our security if this can happen here. I'd expect that outside the wall but here ..." He trailed off for a moment into deep thought.

"They were dressed as workmen. Maybe they weren't even that. Just snuck in a gate."

"Or maybe they are still within our community," Kirk said. "People would be surprised how many commoners and climbers we already have within the Circle. And now traitors, it seems."

"How can that be?"

"I have to have people to run things. Originally, there were only 40 families who truly met our standards. We built hastily but with an eye to expansion of our number. After the *Lyre* sank, we accepted more high-end millionaires to invest — "

"Really, only 40? But New Atlanta is so big!"

"We had to accommodate the AWE garrison and the officers' families. To make the project attractive, our retreat had to be more than a doomsday bunker. To create New Atlanta, we had to put the wall around part of Old Atlanta. For the shops, the greenhouses, the engineers, the warehouses ...everyone who works here, we had to make concessions. Contractors and their families had to be brought inside. Everyone wanted to save a grandmother."

"How did you choose Atlanta in the first place?"

"Originally, the plan was to build a remote community from scratch in South Dakota. Atlanta had the infrastructure we could use: the sewers, the rail hub and the water purification plant. So we built our walled retreat here.

"Since then, I've had people sit in that same chair try to convince me every one of their cousins would be useful to me. I have a pilot for my helicopter and a pilot for my jet and I had to allow both their families inside to secure their loyalty. To accommodate future expansion, there are many buildings within the Circle that stand empty."

Kirk was clearly bragging. All I could think about were all the people beyond the wall without a roof over their heads.

"I have a farm up in Alaska. Every week, the family I hired to take care of the place ask when I'll let them join our greenhouse workers here. Gave them jobs. It's never enough. I take no pleasure in saying no but it's a large part of my life. People are after me on all sides to do something for them. It's almost a daily onslaught."

"Mrs. Rossi called it *noblesse oblige.*

He made a sour face.

I had no sympathy for Kirk. Almost every day this man was offered a chance to change someone's life for the better, to be a hero. He refused as many of those opportunities as he could.

"The logistics of maintaining this city extend far beyond our walls. This is a more delicate situation than you realize. If our security is compromised, the value of our community's investment drains away. I'd appreciate it if you would keep this incident to yourself for now, at least until my wife can investigate. I assure you, Evelyn will get to the bottom of this. She's at church with Eye and Wanda right now. Wanda prays for salvation, Eye prays for a pony and Evelyn's prayers are all imprecatory."

"What's that?"

He smiled. "You've heard of fatwas? Imprecatory prayer is kind of the Christian version: praying for the deaths of one's enemies. When I was courting Evelyn, I loved her uniform and couldn't wait to get her out of it. When I close my eyes and picture her now, I see an angel with a sword, laying waste to God's enemies."

"I thought the poor were supposed to be blessed."

Kirk guffawed. "Well, look around. Obviously not."

When he was done laughing at me, he took on a conspiratorial look. "Evelyn's bent on claiming all of Atlanta for the Select Few one day. With my ticker missing some of its beats occasionally, I do all my warfare with spreadsheets and lawyers."

I managed to keep the revulsion from my face as I said, "Don't worry. I can keep a secret."

"Can you?"

"Certainly."

He smiled. "I appreciate discretion, especially among my staff."

"Uh-huh."

"Especially among my young female staff. You know, when you told me about your part in tracking down the man who stole your town's communal rations, I was appalled at first. Now, when I look at you, I see Evelyn when she was younger and not so ... well, Evelyn. I was very generous to her then, just as I could be very generous to you now."

I stood in a hurry.

"Please don't leave," Kirk said.

"I don't think we have more to discuss, do we? I know what you want. I don't know what kind of arrangement you had with my predecessor — "

"Tanya was very special to me. I was sorry to see her go but — "

"It would be better if you didn't finish that sentence, Mr. Rossi. I'm not available for the games you want to play and you shouldn't be, either."

He let out a long sigh, as if deflating. "Evelyn is a very strong woman, but cold. When we were younger, she always looked happy to see me. Now, she barely looks at me. I'm not a bad guy, Kismet. I'm just very lonely."

"Mr. Rossi, Eye thinks you're a great father."

"I try."

"Try harder."

He looked hurt. I didn't care. Kirk Rossi reminded me too much of Clayton Dobbs.

"You say you're lonely. Monsters are lonely creatures. They hide out in caves, under bridges ... maybe even behind walls and desks and lawyers. You say you're not a bad guy. Are you sure about that?"

I left before he could answer.

CHAPTER TWENTY-NINE

W hen I went for walks with Eye, I kept looking over my shoulder, scanning for my attackers. Before the assault in the arboretum, I hadn't noticed how often men in brown aprons appeared on the street. Sometimes they'd be repairing a downed power line or a solar array. Sometimes they would suddenly appear opposite me on the narrow street. For a second, I was sure it was the man with the walrus mustache. Nerves, I guess.

Walrus mustache or not, I wondered who else might have me under surveillance. "Eye, is that man who just passed us looking back? Is he watching me?"

Sometimes Eye said yes and when I looked back to see the man's face, he'd already disappeared and the girl would laugh, teasing me. "If they look at you, it's because you're pretty!"

Not wanting to scare Eye, I'd explained away my bruised cheek. I told her I slipped on the ladder as I came down in the middle of the night to go to the bathroom.

The situation was not good but I had hope and a new key card. I now had access to the Rossis' living quarters.

I dusted and vacuumed the house with no windows on the first floor. All the furniture was bulky and of a dark wood that did not brighten the gloomy interior in the least. I went about my duties conscientiously for, even in their home, I spotted surveillance cams that could be checking up on me. However, I detected no cameras in Evelyn and Kirk's bedroom.

My breath quickened as I dared to search their closets. In Evelyn's night table drawer I found an M11 handgun. My mother wore the same sidearm every day she was on duty. I left the weapon where I found it. Though it was a tempting find, I worried it would be discovered missing before I had a chance to complete my mission. I went through the pockets of Evelyn's spare uniforms. Each was pressed and perfect. No key card to the Security Center, no luck.

Fearful that I'd set off an alarm, I went back outside into the punishing heat. As I vacuumed the Rossis' pool, surveillance cams followed me. I wanted to jump in fully clothed, just to get a respite. Sweat trickled down my neck. Under my apron, the wet shirt sucked to to my back, cloying like a second skin. Salt stung my eyes. There was something about the feeling in the air, as if the heat was so intense that the Earth's oxygen was burning away.

Even the birds were quiet, like all of nature listened, waiting for the inevitable storm to strike and finally break the tension.

Grammy would have called it tornado weather. I'd never seen a tornado but she had often described the eerie feeling before the weather turns deadly. When my grandmother was my age, she stood in her parents' front yard in Jacksonville. She saw a waterspout pulling boats up from the marina. When a twister made landfall, she ran back to the front door of her house.

"My ears popped," Grammy told me. "The air pressure behind me was so much, I couldn't open the front door to the house. My father staggered around from the back of the house and pulled me away. We jumped into the car. From the back window, I watched my childhood home get ripped up, nothing but splinters and shards, rags and tatters."

I missed Grammy and wondered how she was faring. If she fell, how long before Lisa came to check on her? If Grammy began to starve, would she be too proud to ask for help?

With the failure of my mission imminent, maybe I'd never find out.

The looming storm might come in the form of torrential rain or a hail of bullets.

"Kismet?"

Startled, I jumped. Evelyn stood in the doorway behind me. I was sure she knew I'd searched her room. Soon I'd be back in a CSS interrogation room. This time they'd use the fire hose.

But I was wrong.

"I'm very concerned," Evelyn began. "On the day of your attack, someone in an AWE uniform tampered with the surveillance cameras in the arboretum."

"So there's no way to find out who they were?"

"Whoever it was, she was very careful. I've discussed your account of the events on Sunday with Kirk."

"Oh?"

"You seem surprised."

"Since you didn't mention it, I thought maybe you'd let it go."

"A member of my household staff was attacked within our walls. Of course, I'm not going to let it go. There are bigger security issues here than you and your bruised cheek, Kismet."

"What can I do to help?"

"They disabled the cameras in the arboretum with a spray. As soon as they hit the exit, they split up. They seemed to know where to go to avoid our precautions from tracking them back to whatever hole they came from."

AWE. Always Watching Everywhere. Apparently not.

"I need you to come over to the security center. I've got hours and hours of surveillance recordings for you to watch, first from Sunday and then each hour of every day since. We're going to find this spy in an AWE uniform and her accomplices. As long as they're free, no one in New Atlanta is safe."

"May I go change first? I'm soaked through. This heat — "

"This may take some time. Hurry up, but have a quick shower. Meet me in the garage in twenty minutes."

CSS officers had searched my backpack. I assumed it was Evelyn herself who searched my bag again on my first night in the narrow house. If they'd found the tip of the spear then, Evelyn would have hanged me at the nearest gate as a warning to anyone who might contemplate betrayal.

But the memory stick was always in plain sight, secreted inside the hair clip Chantelle had given me when I arrived at the rendezvous point.

I began to tremble, not just because of what I was about to risk, but because of all that was at stake.

A new thought occurred to me. My sister was working against the Circle as an Intelligence officer. Every day, she faced the possibility of getting arrested and executed. Sissy was up the chain of command. To open that impenetrable steel door for me, my sister might have given the order to have me beaten up.

I stared at the little memory stick. "Maybe you did, Sissy. Maybe you didn't," I said. "This better work. If it doesn't — and if they don't hang us first — I swear I'll kick you hard, right in the baby maker."

CHAPTER THIRTY

Evelyn waited for me in the garage by the door to the Circle's Security and Surveillance Center. She pulled a key card hidden behind her wide white belt that was attached by a gold chain. No wonder I hadn't been able to find a spare key card. She must have had it on her person at all times. So much for my dream of sneaking in where I wasn't supposed to be after midnight.

"Having the AWE center right next door is very convenient," I said.

The door swung open to reveal a short tunnel to the next building. "Its placement wasn't a coincidence. Kirk is a very well-placed and powerful man. The house in which you live was an original, from before the wall. The wall was only halfway through its construction when I insisted this building be placed here. I'm never far from work. Do you know why I work so hard, Kismet? The world is full of moochers who would take everything from us."

Because you have everything and we have nothing, I thought.

When I last saw my sister, she said, "The Select told us that to avoid a civil war, they had to take control. That's how we got sucked deeper into this class war. The people will not revolt because they are poor. We're used to that. We will revolt when we can no longer stand the distance between what little we possess and how much the elite hoard."

Evelyn ushered me through the door. I walked ahead of her through the narrow passage. I couldn't stretch my arms to either side. The dark passageway between buildings reminded me of castles with built-in choke points, made easy for one swordsman to defend.

Medieval architects had no inkling of cyber warfare, though. I just needed to get inside the surveillance hub. The tip of the spear would do the rest.

At the end of the passageway, we walked up a steep ramp that emptied into the middle of a dim room filled with active screens. Every gate of the complex was monitored. The camera feeds flipped every few seconds, scanning faces, looking for troublemakers.

I'm right here, I thought. *No peeking.*

AWE Officers monitored their consoles for surveillance feeds. There seemed to be as many camera feeds from outside the wall as inside. On one screen, several teams of workers unloaded a train that was flanked by greenhouses. Another tracked begging children as they walked alongside a CSS truck somewhere beyond the concrete barrier. From another high angle, a guard absentmindedly picked his nose as he stood beside his guard shack.

I froze in my tracks, transfixed. No wonder Evelyn felt like a god. Her wealth made her omnipotent. Her position made her very nearly omnipresent.

Evelyn tapped me on the shoulder to get my attention. "This room is one of the Circle's secure information hubs, the eyes and ears of Always Watching Everywhere. Somewhere in these recordings, you'll find your attackers."

I looked around the cramped room. No fewer than a dozen AWE officers sat at their consoles, their eyes glued to the shifting images. I finally understood how deeply in the dark I'd been kept. My task suddenly felt like a suicide mission.

When my sister handed me the tiny disc drive, she admitted my mission would not be easy. I would have to get close to powerful people. She claimed she didn't know more details, either. I was to go to a bus stop on a specific street in Atlanta at a certain time of night. A woman named Chantelle would make contact and tell me where to go next.

Looking around the control room, my confidence drained away.

While my mother was in rehab, relearning how to walk, I asked exactly how she lost her leg.

"Wasn't lost," she said. "It was taken. I was on patrol at the edges of a riot. Things seemed to be quietening down when I heard a girl crying. She called out for help. I went down an alley to investigate. I thought I was righteous as Jesus, out to save a civilian. It was dark, no way I could see the tripwire. When the IED blew, I got my eggs scrambled. That's how they got me, but my unit crushed that rebellion. I am an outlier. When you pit a bunch of civilians against an army with a lot of ordnance, bet on the ones with the guns."

It was obvious AWE had all the power and all the weapons. How could the Resistance match their resources? The Circle looked awfully safe to me.

In Campbellford, I had pressed Sissy for more information about what the hack would do.

"For operational security, the less we know about Operation Jericho, the better," Sissy replied.

"Operation Jericho? Snazzy name. But is that really what they teach you in Army Intelligence? That less information is better?"

Sissy smiled. "That's how this world works. You only need to know what I tell you. Be the good little sister and just accept what I'm telling you, okay? Please?"

Grammy needed money and supplies to keep living and my sister had promised both. "I'll do it for Grammy."

"It's for all of us," she said.

Going in with as little information as possible suddenly seemed amazingly stupid.

I was startled as Evelyn raised her voice to address everyone in the room. "What's our motto, team?"

Every officer present replied with gusto and apparent glee, "We are AWE. *We* are what separates us from the animals!"

That was the sort of talk that allowed people to become murder machines. When I closed my eyes, I saw children dead in their parents' arms. The empty stares of corpses were burned into my brain. Those who perished in the ditch died in pain but they did not look surprised. That was the cutting detail that condemned humanity the most.

All I had to fight AWE and the CSS was a memory stick hidden in a hair clip.

CHAPTER THIRTY-ONE

I sat in the control room for hours staring at views from surveillance cameras. The scans zipped through every facet of New Atlanta: the plazas, the quiet and empty streets, each gate, the bustle around the towers.

A junior officer named Michael Baker was assigned to me. When Evelyn left the control room, his eyes followed her for a beat longer than was discreet.

Baker noticed my stare and smirked. "What's she like off duty?"

"I don't live with her in the same house. She's two doors down. If I had to guess, I'd say she's never off duty. She seems the same all the time."

"Awesome and terrifying," he said. "She started out as one of us, you know, worked her way up to Captain of the Guard."

"And married a billionaire."

"Incidental and an opportunity that came with her station. She would have risen through the ranks with him or without him. Everybody in AWE respects Captain Rossi. She has it all because she's worthy and blessed. I once heard her husband admit she's the brains of the operation."

"I'm not surprised."

"She'll protect New Atlanta at all costs. May the Circle be unbroken."

"At all costs? You know you could be one of those costs, right?"

Baker stared at me, his expression blank and stupid. "I don't get what you mean. I'm on the inside and I carry a gun."

He gestured to a feed from beyond the wall. An old man was begging at the gate and getting turned away. "I got no problems, not like them."

I ignored him and went back to pretending to search for the man with the walrus mustache.

Baker was not satisfied. "You want to know something about life here, Miss? When one of us is promoted, Captain Rossi gives a little speech. It's the same speech every time. She always mentions that she wasn't born into the Select but she earned her place. 'We protect our betters. It's how we become better.'"

"Uh-huh."

"You know what else she says?"

"You're going to tell me, I'm sure."

"She says she'd rather die than be one of you again."

"One of me?"

"You're a maid, right? You're not military and you're not rich so you can't be part of the club. You're expendable."

"My parents and sister are all military, Mr. Baker," I said. "They served honorably and with distinction. My mother lost a leg. My sister joined up to save lives. My father trained hundreds of recruits to survive. What you really mean is they weren't lucky enough to draw the same duty as you. Mr. Baker, you've got something in common with your masters. You think you're special because of where you are instead of what you are. Must be comfy."

"Meaning?"

"You could just as easily be out there on a checkpoint searching vehicles for IEDs at the side of a road, sniper bait."

The shifting pale glow from the surveillance screens lit his face. I leaned in close to whisper so only he could hear. "I feel a little sorry for you."

Baker seemed confused before but at the suggestion that someone like me could pity him, he pulled away, obviously furious.

I yanked his wheeled chair back and pulled him to me until my mouth was almost touching his ear. "Listen up, mayonnaise. You're on the happy side of the wall. But that gun that gives you swagger? It's to protect *them*, not you."

He rolled his eyes. "I don't take advice from a housemaid."

"I'm not just that, Mr. Baker. I've seen things so trust me when I tell you, it's not about how macho you feel. The life soldiers choose is one of sacrifice. Sorry to break it to you, but you're no better off than a little Latinx housemaid. Here? Next to people with money and power? You're only here to serve them and make them comfortable. When the revolution comes, *you're* the sacrifice, baby girl."

He rose from his chair and paced a moment before announcing that he was going to "hit the latrine."

Left alone, I pulled out my hair clip, separating the memory stick from its hiding place. I bent beneath the desk and plugged the tip of the spear into the USB port.

I straightened and looked around the room. The other officers on duty had grown used to my presence. They had not noticed my act of sabotage. I went back to pretending to look for my attackers.

The Resistance had invaded in AWE's security systems, ready to hack.

I thought I got away with it, too.

CHAPTER THIRTY-TWO

The night before the full moon, the storm that had been threatening Atlanta hit hard. Old Atlanta got the worst of it. I was to pick up Eye from the Rossis' office tower. In the ballroom near the top of the high-rise, a party was well underway. I was supposed to take Eye home for her bedtime. An AUTONAV car dropped me off out front of the building as thunder rolled and lightning crackled across the sky.

Despite my umbrella, my legs were drenched by the torrential rain before I got to the entrance. An AWE officer checked me in and programmed the elevator to take me to the ballroom. I'd never been in an elevator except for the slow and creaky one at the narrow house. This elevator was quick and smooth. The fast rise was thrilling but the little lurch as it settled on arrival made my stomach flutter.

The doors parted and I was in a world I'd never imagined. To my left, a buffet table was laden with enough food to feed many families for many days. Most of the partygoers weren't even eating. They stood around, drinking and talking as a violin quartet played music for them to ignore.

The servers wore violet vests to match their violet pants and dresses. Every man and woman circulating the party carrying a tray of food wore white gloves. I guessed they were Filipinx.

The attendees were mostly white and dressed in tuxedos and glamorous gowns. A few bearded men wore white thawbs.

Looking around the room at all those soft middles and chattering faces oblivious to looming dangers, I had to smile a little.

The Slow Apocalypse is about to speed up, I thought, *and not for the people it usually hurts.*

My heart picked up its pace as a familiar man and woman stepped out of the throng. The woman wore a mean smile. The man frowned, his forehead an array of flat parallel lines.

I never forget a face. It was Chuck and Marjorie, the people who gave me a ride as far as the diner. Unfortunately, the perverts who wanted to take me home and give me a bath didn't forget a face, either.

"Well, well, well," Chuck said. "It's the liar. You remember this girl, don't you, Marjorie? She's the one who threatened us. What was it she said? That she'd burn us with kerosene?"

"I do remember! This girl stole my fifty dollars."

"The word is *extorted*, Marjorie," I said. "I extorted money from you, and it was only forty dollars."

Chuck looked happy.

"You said you were his paramour," I told Marjorie. "I looked that word up. In your case, it means you're a prisoner to his money."

Her smile faded.

"He'll get rid of you when you get your next wrinkle."

Chuck slapped me across the face. The music wasn't so loud to cover the echo of that slap. The servers looked my way, wide-eyed and concerned. Someone laughed. Mostly, the rest of the partygoers ignored his sudden violence. My cheek was still stinging as I turned back to him and glared.

"Ooh, you've made her mad now, Chuck!" Marjorie tittered. Her laughter was the sort of sound only a stupid human can make, the sort of noise that invites anyone nearby to stick sharp pencils through their eardrums.

"Violence," I said, "is the last resort of weak people who are out of ideas. Given the party, I really thought we'd trade bon mots and witty rejoinders — "

He slapped me again, this time on my sore cheek.

"We were out in the wilderness, enjoying the view when we came upon you," Chuck told me. "Out there on the highway and in the woods was your world. You're in New Atlanta now. The Circle is *my* place. What to do? What to do? You know what? I think I'll have you arrested. Forty dollars and uttering threats? What do you say I arrange it so you get ... what do you think is fair, Marjorie?"

"I don't know. She had me awfully frightened. Expulsion alone is too dangerous. She might prey on others. How about you talk to your friends and throw her in prison indefinitely? At least until she's older and more mature."

The full moon would arrive the next day. Perhaps that's what emboldened me. I pointed to the view from the floor to ceiling windows. "There's a storm coming. It's almost here."

Chuck shrugged. "So?"

"I'm talking about another storm. The one you can't see. When the revolution comes, people like you might want to be on the good side of people like me."

The big man laughed off my threat. "You're boring me."

"I hanged a man. They say the first kill is the hardest. It really wasn't so difficult, not if I dislike someone enough."

Chuck laughed at me. My words were too rushed to convince him but Marjorie looked worried. I slowed down and focused on the weak link.

"Look in my eyes," I told her. "Do you see anything but conviction?"

"Chuck, call the guard. Get them to take her away, please."

I took a step closer to Chuck. Startled, he backed away quickly. He looked worried, but not so much that I'd avoid arrest.

Marjorie's eyes were wide and wet, not a little horrified. "Does he order you around? I've heard a lot about men of the Select Few. We don't hear much about their trophy wives and mistresses but I can guess. Does he make you get young girls for him?"

"I ... I ... uh ... " Marjorie trembled and looked away.

"Not much of a denial there, Marge. Does Chuck tell you what to wear and say and think? He looks like the kind of guy who has to pay for a lady's company. Maybe Chuck calls it an allowance or gifts, but that's what it is. You're quite attractive. No way a woman like you would be with a guy like him unless you had to be. Scared of starving? Do you worry where you'll end up when he's done with you? What happens when your looks slip? What does Chuck have in mind for your future?"

"It's not like that ... " she replied in a small voice — *too small a voice.* "Please stop. You're awful."

"Says the woman who was just applauding my brutalization at the hands of Chuck's thugs."

She wiped a tear from her cheek as if she was hastily erasing a mistake.

I persisted. "Do you dream that one day soon he'll drop dead and you'll finally be free? Don't feel bad, Marjorie. We all want to be free of some horror or other."

Unable to meet Chuck's withering glare, she gave another slight, unconvincing shake of her head. I felt sorry for her. I was a spy but Marjorie wore a mask, too. She struggled to look like a besotted idiot in love. Her mask had slipped.

Chuck caught her look, too. When he understood what she really thought of him, his face fell.

With tears slipping down her cheeks, Marjorie turned and ran as fast as anyone can in high heels and a mermaid dress. I assumed she was headed for the bathroom. Chuck ordered me to stay where I was and chased after her, maybe to argue, perhaps to chastise her.

I was headed for jail. Or maybe I was bound for a ditch before Operation Jericho went into effect. Defiance, even in the face of the inevitable, felt good. Without my knives, hurtful, truthful words were perhaps the only way a person like me could hurt a man like Chuck.

I have no illusions that I would have successfully bullied my way out of the clutches of Chuck's assorted henchmen and jailers. It wasn't cleverness that gave me my escape. It was my job as Eye's nanny that got me away from Chuck before he returned.

An AWE officer appeared only long enough to scan my face.

"Kismet Beatriz? You don't belong here. Come back to the elevator. The Rossi family is expecting you in Mr. Rossi's office. Top floor."

I hurried after my unwitting savior. He turned a key and pushed the elevator button. I rose to the selected floor and out of my enemy's clutches.

I breathed a sigh of relief, thankful for the respite. It would not last long.

CHAPTER THIRTY-THREE

My heart was still pounding as the elevator doors parted. I wiped the sweat from my brow and stepped into an anteroom. Chuck had ordered me to stay, as if I were a dog. I marveled at the arrogance of a person so sure his orders would be followed that he expected me to hang around to get arrested. He must have figured he could get me later. Once within the Circle, where could I escape?

One disaster at a time, I thought.

Grammy would say, "God doesn't send you more than you can handle, but what does God know about us little people? He expects too much and most of us are too weak to carry that kind of load, if you ask me."

Since the funerals, Grammy told me that same thing every day, several times a day. She had a lot of memorable observations I loved, but as her mind slipped, she held onto some more than others. It was as if she were clinging to a security blanket, trying to hold on to what she was. Those little bits of wisdom had become all she was reduced to.

Her memory loss was slow at first. That was the worst time, when she could see her erasure coming. "I'm losing my marbles, Kismet! I miss them, but I almost can't wait until I won't miss them anymore."

I stood in the anteroom on the edge of a panic attack. Cold sweat beaded on my forehead. My breath was short and shallow, like a hummingbird. I needed to get back to Grammy. I wanted to run.

No wonder people who could never join the Select Few aspired to their station. There were even commoners who idolized them. Theirs was a faint hope for shelter, a dream that after a long fall, somehow they would somehow land safely.

I was very close to being exposed. The closer we crept toward the full moon, the more precarious my position seemed. Was Chuck, at that same moment, ordering his goons to search the building for me? Almost certainly.

Kirk appeared in a doorway. "Kismet? Are you not feeling well?"

I cleared my throat. "The elevator," I said. "It's fast. My stomach ... "

"It's not that fast. Are you claustrophobic?"

"Sure, that could be it. A little."

"Come. I've got the best view of the city. This'll clear your head."

I followed him into a huge office with floor-to-ceiling windows. Eye lay asleep on a couch beside a massive desk. Evelyn stood in silhouette against a raging sky. As thunder rolled overhead, lightning struck Old Atlanta again and again.

"Magnificent, isn't it?" Evelyn said. "What's that old joke? This light show brought to you by God, maker of just about everything! The cannibal class will not sleep easy tonight."

Before I could stop myself, I blurted, "Cannibal class?"

"A little joke among us," Kirk explained. "All those people beyond our walls would crawl over each other, kill each other to stand where you're standing right now."

Maybe not each other, I thought. *Maybe you.*

"Hard to believe we had another summer of drought and now this," Evelyn said. "There's going to be a lot of flooding. Maybe we'll get forty days and forty nights and all the rats will drown."

I heard relish in Evelyn's tone. To her, the people in the camps were just vermin. People like me wished we had money to feel safe. For Evelyn Rossi to feel safe, we all had to die.

She put an arm around my shoulder. The alcohol on her breath told me she was not just a little drunk. "Quite the view, isn't it?"

"Yes, ma'am."

"Doesn't it make you grateful?" she asked. "No worries about a leaky roof, the privacy of your own room ... food. When I was just a little younger than you, I lived at home with five brothers. My mother died in childbirth. My father resented me for it. Now they're all gone. Some died honorably in war. One went to war and came home to kill himself. The youngest died of starvation. Yet here I stand."

"Queen of the castle!" Kirk toasted her with a raised glass of wine.

"They thought I was weak," she added. "My father, my brothers ... you know what they didn't understand? I was patient. They picked on me but all I had to do was wait them out. One by one, they all fell down. Ordinary people have families. That's nice, but I have a legacy. No, a *dynasty*."

"An *empire*, my love," Kirk said.

Evelyn glanced back at her sleeping daughter. "An empire that will last a thousand years. We are the clear blue sky and the cannibal class is just cloud formations ... so temporary they're almost silly."

She gestured toward Old Atlanta. "All *that* is going away."

"You rose and rose," Kirk added. "Admirable. I spotted your potential from the moment we met."

"Please, Kirk. Speak with elegance. Use your English accent."

"You know I don't feel comfortable putting on airs. I'm not ashamed to come from here."

"Bad form! Please, Kirk! Be sexy for me."

Kirk sighed. "Beastly, sorry, madam! I do declare, we should let the nanny fetch our offspring and return to the cotillion."

"Now you're just making fun of me," Evelyn pouted.

"Gently," he said, "but yes. Let's get back to the party and have some claret."

"Let's stay and watch the storm for another few minutes. I do love a good storm, especially from up here. What's the quote from Isaiah about storms and our safety within the Circle?"

"You're the family's Bible scholar, honey."

"It's ... um." She finished her drink and gestured to the angry sky. "I've got it! I've got it! It will be a shelter and shade from the heat of the day, a refuge and a hiding place from the storm and the rain."

Still sweating, I blurted a question I shouldn't have asked, "Don't most of the people in those camps share your religion, Mrs. Rossi?"

Evelyn removed her arm from my shoulder, stared at me and swayed. "He works in mysterious ways. No one can pretend to know the mind of God but I have a few guesses. Maybe they believe, but not strongly enough. Not everybody goes to heaven. If the cannibal class were among the blessed, they'd be up here drinking with me."

I said nothing. She leaned closer, grabbed my wrist and shook my arm. "Right?"

"Yes, ma'am," I said.

"Or maybe we just arrived here under our own power," Kirk suggested.

Said the guy born with every advantage and a ton of money, I thought.

"You're lucky to be here," Evelyn told me. "You know that, don't you?"

"Yes, ma'am."

"You're not jealous, are you? Well? Are you?"

"No, ma'am."

But I was.

The tempest ravaged Old Atlanta's refugee camps, homeless shelters and detention centers. If not for that storm, Operation Jericho would not have ended as it did. Evelyn would attribute her fate and mine to God's caprice. I prefer to blame the end of this story on the Law of Unintended Consequences.

I gathered Eye in my arms and walked to the elevator. An AWE guard was waiting. For a second or two, I thought I was caught again.

Kirk leaned in behind me to push the button for the underground garage. "There's a car waiting for them downstairs. Make sure they get there, will you? Apparently, our nanny's heart goes pitty-pat in elevators."

With the Rossis' child in my arms and an escort, I got out of the building and into the back seat of the AUTONAV car without anyone stopping me.

Under a heavy curtain of rain, traffic was slow. As we inched past the front of the building, a small crowd gathered in the tower lobby. AWE officers were scanning faces and IDs. I didn't see Chuck, but I was pretty sure they were looking for me.

Eye stirred in my arms and sat up. "That party was so boring, I fell asleep. Only old people music." She used her proper English accent out of a dead sleep. I guessed her indoctrination into the Select Few was complete.

I was wrong.

The girl said something more but the torrent increased. Rain drummed on the roof, drowning her out. I pointed to my ears and yelled, "Sorry! Can't hear you!"

Eye smiled, put her arms around my neck and pulled me closer. "I said, tomorrow. Just one more day to the full moon! You must be excited."

I pulled away, in shock, not knowing what to say. Somehow the plans had been leaked. Surely, Operation Jericho was doomed. A wave of nausea rushed through me.

Eye smiled and she waved for me to lean closer again. "Tanya would have done it, but you had to bring the tip of the spear. She wouldn't tell me what it was. Did you stick it where it needed to go?"

"Tanya told you?"

Eye suddenly looked wise beyond her years. "To get you in, she had to go. It was a sacrifice, but after tomorrow, everything's going to get better. Don't worry. AWE may mean Always Watching Everywhere, but that can't be true. The Resistance is everywhere. They can't catch us all."

"But, your family! And the things you said!"

"I'm a kid, not an idiot. If we don't bend, we'll break. My parents don't understand this is for the best. If we don't share, it's all gonna get taken away, anyway."

Such a clever spy I was, outdone by a child. "I don't know what to say anymore."

"You don't have to say anything. I assume you've done your part by now."

She turned to watch New Atlanta slip by. I couldn't fathom how casual she was about the upheaval that would soon come. She glanced at me, squeezed my hand and leaned in again to be heard. "I'm not betraying my parents. That's what you're thinking but you're wrong. I'm saving them. When the revolution comes, the people who aren't on the right side of history will get buried beneath its heavy tread."

"Is that a quote from something?"

Eye shrugged. "Just quoting my mentor."

"Who?"

"Juanita."

"*Who?*"

"My parents didn't raise me. Juanita did. She taught me everything, including the tough parts of the French Revolution. Juanita says this is my chance to save Father and Mother from the guillotine."

"Wanda?"

Eye gave a huge smile, relishing my confusion and surprise. "Juanita is her real name. Father's family insisted she change it. That's our little secret. I've known her real name since I was nine. Wanda is her slave name."

The kid's right, I thought. *The Resistance is everywhere.*

The law of unintended consequences had struck again. Evelyn and Kirk allowed the help to raise their child. Their daughter was inoculated against indoctrination by the Select Few.

Eye spoke with the confidence only idiots, visionaries and the innocent can possess. "When the time comes, I'll explain everything to Mother in a way she'll have to understand."

"How's that?"

"I'll look her straight in the eye and say, 'The wolf will live with the lamb, the leopard will lie down with the goat, the calf and the lion and the yearling together; and a little child will lead them.' Mother does love to quote Isaiah."

Little Eileen Rossi was not about to give up her princess status among the Select Few, after all. She planned to lead us all, rich and poor alike.

CHAPTER THIRTY-FOUR

As the day of the full moon dawned over New Atlanta, I worried the hack had failed. My nerves felt like they were stretching out, taut as guitar strings. Grammy used to call this condition "discombobulation." I think that was one of the first words she lost as her marbles rolled away.

Wanda appeared at my shoulder and whispered to me as I washed the dishes after lunch. "Eye told you about me."

I nodded. "Why didn't you tell me you were one of us?"

"You're a maid. I'm a maid. We're all 'one of us.' Doesn't change the fact that AWE is everywhere."

"I saw all the screens they have to watch. There aren't enough of them to catch everything. If they were as powerful as they pretend, there wouldn't be graffiti on the Circle's walls."

"The graffiti is on the outside. Do that inside the Circle and they'll track you back to your house and drag you out for a beating."

"Maybe not after today."

"Don't count your chickens," she whispered. "Eye is good at keeping secrets but she got ahead of herself telling you anything. If the Resistance fails, our only hope will be that little girl, acting and talking like one of them until she can get into a position to make reforms and turn things around."

"You don't think this'll work? Did I risk my life for nothing?"

She brought a finger to her lips. "Hard to say. Heard a rumor there's big doings outside the wall today but it could turn into another Portland."

Don't talk to me about Portland, I thought.

"The storm knocked out all the power and two shelters flooded."

"Were people hurt?"

"No more than usual, I don't think, but it's got people especially riled up. The weather's clearing but they got themselves in a humid mood. Trouble's in the air. Be ready for it."

"Ready how? What should I do? Make sure my bladder is empty?"

"If you have to evacuate, that wouldn't be a bad thing, would it? If it comes to that, I'll drive you. There's a seed vault across from Gate 12. If needs must be, wait in the alley beside it and I'll come find you. I can get you out. Fair warning: If you aren't there, I'm just gonna keep driving."

"Sounds like you're expecting big trouble, Wanda."

"People are some riled, but the Select are motivated to hold on to everything they've got. It's going to depend on the parrots. If they see there's no way to continue, the battle might go our way."

"What about Eye and her parents?"

"The Rossis got contingency plans."

Wanda surprised me by reaching into her apron and pulling out my knives. Without a word, she placed them in a drawer with the utensils. "If things go badly, I imagine you'll want these should you find yourself on the other side of the wall."

Seeing the weapons my parents gave me made me tear up a little. "Thank you."

"This is the most I can do. If today goes sideways, Eye is my first priority. If you give her or me up, I'll give up everyone I know in my cell. Do you understand?"

I had a lot of questions but I knew better than to ask them. I nodded and went back to drying dishes. Wanda left to go about her work.

I cursed my sister under my breath a few times, but there was no energy behind it, no real hate in my heart. Only fear.

It wasn't her fault that I found myself standing in the Rossis' kitchen. "Dancing on the precipice of danger" is what Daddy would have called it.

"It's where the excitement is," Mama would always reply. "It's where the doers are."

That exchange came up a few times, always on the nights before deployment. I never wanted them to leave. They just shrugged their shoulders and asked, "If we don't serve, how are you going to pay the bills, Kismet?"

So I played the role of the dutiful daughter, stayed home to take care of Grammy and waved goodbye to my mother, father and sister.

The last time, only one came back. I told my grandmother my parents were dead. I told her everything I knew about the Portland strike, sparing no details.

The propapundits called it the Portland Uprising. Perpetrated by terrorists, they said. First, we were told that it was Resistance that set off the bomb that had murdered my parents. Then someone of the nuclear committee leaked an admission that it was our new government that did the deed.

General Elliot Ramundsen was not a noble whistleblower. His announcement was not an apology. It was a warning to resistance groups and grassroots organizers across the country.

"It was a tough call," the general said, "but leadership is about making tough calls. With the blessing of the Select Few, I called in the nuclear strike. For the longevity of the Republic, Portland needed what I'd call a brushback pitch."

According to Ramundsen, the city's tragic sacrifice at the hands of cruel people was worth the weight of sin and loss. The warning worked, too. Plans for more austerity protests were abandoned.

"These seditious bastions of a failed governmental model must be excised from our national discourse," the general proclaimed. "Weak liberalism is a pox on our country and it is in its death throes. Let the erasure of Portland and its mistakes serve as a warning to anyone who ponders any challenge to our nation and our way of life."

Many people went quiet, waiting to see how bad the blowback might be before committing to what was right and what was wrong. As condemnations of the strike on Portland poured in from across the country and around the globe, Ramundsen doubled down. He even named the other cities at the top of his target list. He called Austin, Berkeley, Sacramento and Dearborn nests of traitors. My parents were not traitors. They were serving their country and got in the way.

General Ramundsen was assassinated by his own bodyguards. As my sister observed, "The people in charge didn't take that as a hint at constructive feedback."

Through the magic of propaganda, the general's death was used to justify his actions. The Select made their monster into a martyr. His assassins, all decorated military personnel, went to their execution after a perfunctory trial. They never retracted the assertion they made upon their arrest: They were not part of some left-wing conspiracy. They'd killed Ramundsen for their fallen comrades.

People abandoned their homes to flee those cities. For fear that the committee would strike again, all protests and marches were called off. The oligarch's seizure of power seemed complete.

It seemed no one could defy those in charge but my sister knew better. "The Resistance is not dead," Sissy told me. "It just looks dead because it's buried underground. When you go into New Atlanta, set your jaw and grit your teeth. When we dig ourselves out of the grave they put us in, they're going to regret even touching the shovel."

At our parents' graves, Sissy hugged me and said, "When we dared to complain that we were starving and dying and needed the basics of what governments are for, they said ours was a 'grievance-fueled ideology.' It wasn't then, but it sure is now."

"When you call, I'll do what you need done. For Mama and Daddy."

"For you, me and Grammy," she replied.

A thousand small decisions had led me to this day. If the government had not cut benefits to the families of veterans, maybe I'd still be in Campbellford. If Clayton Dobbs hadn't stolen the town's food supplies, I would not have condemned him to death. When I didn't flinch at that traitor's hanging, Sissy got her first inkling that her little sister might be useful to the cause.

But the past didn't matter anymore. There was no safe place. There was nothing for me in Campbellford except a charming old lady who might not even know my name when I saw her again.

The second time I had to remind Grammy that Daddy and Mama were dead, I skimped on the details. The third time, I cried. After that, I humored her and pretended that they were still out west helping to fight wildfires, evacuating civilians and saving lives. Then I had to pretend they were still sending us enough money to feed us.

Life was easier when I lied to myself. I often fantasized that Portland was just more lies meant to scare us. I told myself that one day I'd look up and Mama would limp into our little kitchen. She'd be carrying a big bag of groceries. She'd say. "Everything is back to bingo, bongo, tickety-boo."

Daddy would say, "You're still dreaming, Kismet. Ask yourself, could any of this be real? Wake up, Kissy! Can't be real, right? We're right here."

But I wasn't dreaming. The horror was real.

I didn't get a chance to escape New Atlanta before the next storm hit. As I put the last of the dishes away, two AWE officers appeared in the doorway.

"Kismet Beatriz?" It was Michael Baker, the AWE officer I had annoyed.

"You know who I am. Why play around?"

"Because I don't know you and I don't want to know you. You're under arrest."

My jaw went slack. I didn't know what was supposed to occur when Operation Jericho went into effect. This wasn't the end I pictured. I squeezed my eyes tight and asked myself, *Is this real?*

I opened my eyes. The officers still trained their pistols on me. My parents' gifts to me, so precious to me, stayed in the utensil drawer, useless.

The AWE officers did not carry handcuffs. I hadn't noticed that before. They had no use for them. They either beat their prisoners into submission, banished them or executed them outright.

Baker and his partner grabbed me roughly by the arms and escorted me down to the garage. As we arrived at the door to the Security Center, sirens began to sound across New Atlanta. It was a long mournful howl, rising and falling. I took some small pleasure in the nervous look Baker and his partner exchanged as the alarm reached us.

"Something's up," I said.

"Whatever it is, I doubt you'll live to see it," Baker replied.

Operation Jericho had begun too late to save me.

CHAPTER THIRTY-FIVE

Evelyn waited for me in the Security and Surveillance Center. "Well, if it isn't the social climber. Of course, your intentions were never really social, were they?"

"I don't know what you mean."

"An hour ago, a riot erupted at two detention camps," she said. "Now the Circle is in lockdown. Whatever trouble is brewing, we're going to quash it."

"I don't know anything about trouble at the detention camps."

Evelyn stalked back and forth a moment. Everyone in the control room stared at me.

"Tend to business," Evelyn said in a low voice. Her staff snapped back to their duties.

"Bad day?" I asked.

"Punch up 27, exterior," Evelyn ordered. She pointed at a nearby screen. "They say criminals return to the scene of the crime. He didn't come willingly."

I stared. It was Picasso, hanging dead from Gate 27's parapet.

"The CSS caught up to this rebel last night. He shot and killed two officers before he was shot. He died of blood loss in an alley between burned-out apartment buildings in Chamblee."

"And CSS *still* hanged Picasso?" I asked.

"They may not know art, but they know what they like," Evelyn replied.

A chuckle went around the room but I didn't see the humor in it.

"Thirty minutes ago, all the gates and security doors opened at those camps. As of about twenty minutes ago, it looks like all of Old Atlanta is on the march. They're streaming our way."

"I've been washing dishes."

Evelyn slapped me across the face, hard. I'd been slapped a lot lately. My cheek burned but I pretended she'd had no effect.

"Feel better?" I asked. "I don't know anything about your camps opening up. If slapping improves the situation, I live to serve."

She gave an ugly smile. "I'm sure you didn't have anything to do with the hack of CSS security. That's a separate system from AWE."

"So what does this have to do with me?"

"Where's your hair clip? I don't think I've ever seen you without your little black hair clip?"

"It broke," I said.

"I found part of it." Evelyn held up the little memory stick Sissy had dubbed the tip of the spear.

"When the security doors opened in the detention centers, I ordered a sweep of our systems as a precaution. Mr. Baker checked his station. It's the only console where you sat to watch the surveillance recordings. *You* opened a back door to our systems. God knows what havoc you might have given us if we hadn't found it in time."

I shrugged. "Maybe Baker put it there. He doesn't seem like a very nice guy."

He growled behind me and punched me in my left kidney so hard I dropped to my hands and knees, gasping at the pain.

"Who sent you?" Baker demanded.

I had no illusions I could stand up to torture but I could mislead them and stall for time. "Two people who wanted to be peacekeepers, Rich and Kacy."

"Who?"

"Rich and Kacy Beatriz ... my parents." It wasn't so far from the truth.

"A lie," Evelyn said. "I read your scan. Your parents are dead."

"Their deaths brought me here. The Select Few murdered them. They were just collateral damage to you. Not to me."

Baker stepped on my left hand and pressed down with a heavy boot. I stifled a scream and bit down on my lip until I tasted blood.

"I trusted you with my daughter, climber!" Evelyn yelled.

"And I love her," I said.

"Climbers will say anything."

"My love is real. Do you know why Eye is so great? She's not you."

Baker hauled me up by the hair as Evelyn drew back to slap me across the face again.

"Captain!" An AWE officer rose from her seat in front of a bank of monitors. "Breach!"

Evelyn straightened and turned from me. "Where?"

"Gate 2 is open."

"Shut it."

"I already tried," the officer replied. "I'm locked out."

"Gate 16 is opening, too," another called out. "I'm shut out, too."

Another officer raised his hand as if he was in a classroom. "Gate 8, opening on its own." He added darkly, "That's the closest entrance to the horde coming from the refugee camp. The hack must still be active. She opened a door we can't close."

Evelyn scanned the screens as more steel gates began to rise. "Gilhorn! Can we cut power to the gates to contain this?"

"Not from here. It would have to be done manually at the gates."

"Do it."

Gilhorn picked up a phone and immediately put it back into his control board. "The lines to the gates are dead. As far as the guards on each gate know, their gate is open because we opened it from here."

"Radio them!"

"It's jammed, ma'am." A murmur shivered through the control room. I wasn't alone in my fear anymore and that was oddly comforting.

"Get out there!" Evelyn shouted. "All of you, grab a vehicle and get to as many gates as you can to close them manually. Gilhorn, coordinate everyone's assignment. We have to get back into lockdown before those climbers get inside."

Her staff rose as one to follow her orders but she held one AWE officer back and handed her the memory stick. "Brody, they've found an exploit in our system. Try to figure out how much damage they've done. I'm not sure how deep this compromise goes."

Brody nodded. "That will take some time, Captain."

"Then you better start now." Evelyn turned back to me. "What have you done, Kismet?"

"Surprisingly little," I admitted. "Something of this magnitude takes the work of many people working cooperatively to achieve a goal that will benefit the most people."

"A socialist's dream of terrorism."

"*Mm* ... no. Military precision."

I thought she would hit me again. Instead, she stepped so close, she breathed on my face. "I should never have allowed you to weasel your way into our lives."

"What makes it worse for you? That the Circle is about to be invaded or that it's happening on your watch?"

"Captain!" Brody called.

"News already?"

"Not exactly, but something odd outside Gate 12. Check the street feed from Old Atlanta, ma'am."

Evelyn whirled to take in the screens as Brody punched up more surveillance feeds of the streets beyond the wall. On most of the screens, people of Old Atlanta shuffled down the middle of the street. Outside Gate 12, the crowds kept to the sides of the street.

"What are they up to?" Evelyn asked.

"I don't know, Captain," Brody replied nervously, "but every gate is open now. The rabble is still on the outside, as if they're waiting for something. The parrots are skirmishing but we don't have enough of them to defend every gate equally."

Evelyn, pale and shaking with rage, asked me what was coming.

"This is interesting, isn't it?" I said.

Baker tightened his grip and shook me by the hair. "Talk!"

"You know your Bible, Evelyn," I said. "Job is a fascinating story of pain and reward. One detail that always struck me was that when Job gets the bad news of all he has lost, one messenger arrives with the bad news, and then another and another, all talking over each other. When God strikes you down, he doesn't play around. He's got quite a flair for drama, doesn't He?"

"This isn't God."

"Are you sure? If you were still blessed, could this happen to you?"

A signal came up on the screen that was relayed to the area around Gate 12. The screen read:

EVACUATE SECTOR 12.
   EVACUATE SECTOR 12
   IMMEDIATELY.
   THIS IS NOT A DRILL.

"It's going out over the public address system," Brody said. "The hack makes it look as if the warning is coming from here. No way to tell our people to ignore it."

"We don't want our people to ignore it," Evelyn said. "That's where the first breach of our defenses will come. We've got to move, contain and eradicate."

Contain and eradicate, I thought. *God, how she hates us.*

"Brody, stay here and figure out a way to regain control of our systems. Baker, bring the girl. Whoever's leading this revolution may pause a moment when they see we have their spy. We might be able to use that."

"I doubt that will help you, Evelyn," I said. "How many soldiers would you sacrifice to get the Circle back? That's probably how many they'll sacrifice to take it. There are many more lives to save on their side of the wall."

"You people," Baker said. "Portland wasn't enough for you? You're just another bunch of stupid beggars looking for handouts. Jesus, what more could it take for you to learn — "

"We did learn, Michael," I replied. "The Portland protests were about begging for justice. The marches that scared you so much were about closing the gap between the few up and the many down. Right or left, what we all had in common was poverty and the love of our families."

Baker sneered. "What did you learn after we wiped out a city of malcontents with a nuke?"

"We learned that the next march had to be on a city the Select Few would not nuke. You took away our homes so now we're coming to yours for shelter."

"We've got the firepower," Evelyn said. "We'll keep the climbers out."

"This is Operation Jericho," I said. "Your precious Circle will be broken."

Evelyn pulled the pistol from her holster. "I promise you'll never see that. Now move!" She cursed at me all the way to the car.

Wanda and Eye stood in the garage. Eye looked shocked that her mother was pointing a gun at my head. Wanda didn't seem the least surprised.

"Get Eye to the panic room!" Evelyn ordered. "And my husband, too. Where's Kirk?"

"He's at the tower. I tried to get through to him but the phones don't work. They're just static."

"Get to the panic room."

Wanda bobbed her head and ushered Eye toward the door to her parents' private abode. The girl looked back, her eyes wet.

If Operation Jericho failed, what would become of Eye? What would happen to her if the invasion of New Atlanta succeeded?

CHAPTER THIRTY-SIX

I sat in the back seat with Baker and Evelyn sat behind the wheel. She tried to radio her team in the security bunker but received no answer.

"All signals are scrambled, Captain," Baker observed.

"Yes, someone is very thorough."

I wondered where my sister was. She could be colluding with teams of hackers, spinning more impenetrable webs of deceit.

Evelyn and Kirk could have enjoyed their wealth and power and still allowed ordinary people to live as they once did. Having a billion dollars must be a comfort, but what drove a person to go after the next billion and the next billion and the billion after that? The answer to that question would have to remain a mystery.

When we arrived in Sector 12, Baker pushed me out of the car ahead of him, training his pistol on me. The Home Depot was behind me to the left. AWE's Officer Training Academy stood to my right. We were in a large square built to accommodate trucks that made large deliveries. The square served as the academy's parade ground when big trucks weren't rumbling through.

The streets inside the Circle were so empty they echoed. It was as if the residents had disappeared. They had either evacuated to other areas within New Atlanta or hid in their underground bunkers.

Through the gate, the crowd along either side of the street peered back at us, an odd and hauntingly silent vigil. They were men, women, and children of varying ages, all in ragged and dirty clothes. They looked neither angry nor sad. If I had to pin it down, I'd say their expressions were a mixture of expectant and resolute. Someone would surely die, but I detected no fear beyond that gate. These people had little to lose.

Evelyn slowly turned and I followed her gaze. A long low concrete building opposite the gate was punctuated by loading docks: the Circle's armory.

"Oh, no ... " Evelyn whispered.

She stalked toward Gate 12 and ordered the guard to close the gate manually. However, no guard appeared.

Six AWE officers were gathered on the parapet above the gate. Not wanting to tip her hand, she pointed at one to come to her. A fit man with graying hair bobbed his head and rushed down a ladder. He met her halfway to the gate. "Stevenson, ma'am. Orders, Captain?"

"There's no one in the shack, Lieutenant. Report!" Evelyn demanded.

"I didn't know her, ma'am, but she was a regular on the shift. As soon as we saw the mob of climbers coming up the street, I went down to the gate myself to close it. She walked out into the crowd, disappeared into it."

"You should have shot her for desertion."

"I was preoccupied in the shack, ma'am. The lever is broken clean off and the wheels are jammed with some kind of resin. We tried to call it in but — "

"But the radio's jammed, I know." She glanced back at me. "We've been hacked and infiltrated by climbers and their sympathizers, apparently. Tell me what I don't know."

"I sent a runner to get an LRAD but they're in use two gates over."

"I knew we shouldn't have cheaped out. I told the council every gate should have a sound cannon."

After Portland, the Select thought they were safe. They assumed we'd given up. That was the only way we could win. They had to beat us down so hard they were sure we couldn't get up again. Appearing weak was our only advantage and continuing to resist in secret was our only defense.

I wondered if the guard who sabotaged the gate's mechanisms was the same woman who'd watched me get beat up. If so, I decided to forgive her.

"What are you smiling at?" Baker growled.

"Entropy. It's ... inevitable."

The radio on Evelyn's belt crackled to life. It was Brody. "Security Central to Captain Rossi! I've reestablished communications. They're using our own gear against us. I unjammed the jammer."

"Roger that," Evelyn replied. "So you can undo the hack?"

"Uh, no, ma'am. I just unplugged *our* jammer. Over."

"Seriously?" Exasperated, Evelyn made a *tsk* sound. "We're chasing our tails and comin' up all elbows. Order to all AWE guards! Close your gates! Relay that to everyone, Brody! And get hold of CSS, too. We may need outside help."

"The CSS is overrun with troubles in the camps. Climbers have already rushed through Gates 5, 10, 11, 23 and 27, ma'am."

"Coordinated attacks," Baker said. "Maybe lining up on either side of the street was a diversion, Captain. Looks like we've been duped so they'd squeeze in elsewhere."

Evelyn ordered Baker to shut his mouth and yelled into her radio. "Close the rest of the gates. Prepare to contain and eradicate! We'll drive them out."

A moment passed and Evelyn frowned. "Brody? Acknowledge?"

"A new alert just came through on my screen." Brody's voice trembled. "The hack is still active. They're pouring in, Captain. I could unplug everything but then we'll be blind. The climbers are already in the street outside, ma'am. I can hear them marching. I'm alone here and I'm not sure what to do."

"That's why you have orders. Stay calm. We haven't lost anything yet. What's the new alert from the hack?"

"It says firefighting teams should report to Sector 12, ma'am."

Rossi glanced at the gate and considered for a beat. Then she smiled. "Yes! Send fire engines immediately. They're one of the few kinds of vehicles in the Circle that are big enough to block Gate 12. Tell the fire teams to get their asses over here and block the gate immediately."

She turned to Stevenson and tossed her head toward the guards atop the parapet. "You locked and loaded, Lieutenant?"

"I've got five parrots in their perches, ma'am. They've got three mags each. I don't like the math of firing into that crowd, Captain. I'd suggest negotiating."

"Negotiating?"

"They've got all elderly out front. Veterans are at least the first few dozen rows back."

"What?"

"Vets, ma'am. Ribbons and medals on their chests."

My father once told Sissy and me about a battle tactic from an old war. I couldn't remember if it was Iran or Iraq that sent children forward first, shock troops to give the opposing side pause. I like to think Sissy remembered that story and inverted the tactic for Operation Jericho.

It *did* give the parrots pause. Unfortunately, so determined was she to stand her ground, an appeal to decency would not stop Evelyn Rossi. She remained eager to defend her castle to the last.

"There are children out there, too, ma'am," Stevenson reported. "Suppose we find out what they want? This might be solved with a few more rations or — "

"If the climbers didn't want their kids shot, they shouldn't have brought them to my gates, Lieutenant."

A chill ran up my spine. By his face, I wondered if Lt. Stevenson felt that same cold frisson.

CHAPTER THIRTY-SEVEN

A siren rose in the distance as the first fire truck roared through the Circle's narrow streets.

Evelyn smiled in cruel defiance. "The climbers are not getting through this gate, do you hear me?"

But Operation Jericho had many more moving parts than I could have guessed. The hack was a well-coordinated attack. Other vehicles with large engines were on their way. However, that sound did not come from within the Circle.

The crowd lining the street beyond the gate turned their heads away from us, peering to see what was coming. A murmur wound among them. As if they were one organism, the people of Old Atlanta pulled back from the gate. Mothers and fathers stepped in front of their children and turned their backs to the wall.

One of the guards above the gate shouted, "Incoming!" Then he began to fire his weapon. The others joined in.

An AUTONAV truck appeared on the street beyond the gate. There was no driver, of course. The guards' only hope was to disable the vehicle using rifle fire. The engines were in the undercarriage so they fired at the tires.

Screams rose from the crowd and many flattened to avoid getting hit by ricochets. No one ran.

Evelyn raced toward the shack. "Stevenson! Help me! We've got to get the tire spikes up!"

"I told you! It's disabled!" Stevenson yelled back.

"We have to try!"

The first truck punched through Gate 12 like a fist, blowing past Evelyn and barreling toward me at top speed. The truck's sensor must have saved me because the vehicle swerved at the last moment, barely missing Baker.

The AUTONAV clipped the front fender of the vehicle we'd taken to get there. The car spun, narrowly missing my captor. Cursing, Baker yelped and took a few quick steps to his right to avoid getting hit by the car.

Daddy taught me how and where to hit a man with elbows and knees so it counted. "You gotta deal with the weapon before you deal with the man," he told me.

I grabbed Baker's pistol. Struggling to wrench it from his grasp would only get me shot in the face. I twisted it back so the muzzle pointed at his head.

Baker wisely took his finger off the trigger and pulled back to punch me in the face.

My first strike was to his throat. That surprised him. My kick to his shin surprised him more but it was the second elbow to his throat that caught him just so. It was a solid jolt to his airway and jangled his nervous system.

Daddy had been an excellent instructor but Mama instilled in me the importance of being savage when necessary.

"Remember how we taught you to do a high jump?" Mama once said. "How you have to drive your knee up to get elevation? A proper knee to the groin is like the first part of a high jump, all the energy coming straight up, like you're on springs, baby. Go for elevation, drive that knee up, high and hard so you achieve liftoff. Do it right and your opponent will have to open his mouth to pee."

Mama was right. The guard's eyes bugged out on impact. With

adrenaline coursing through my body, my legs really did feel as if they were on springs.

Two more trucks narrowly missed us as I punched the base of his throat for good measure.

Gasping in pain, Baker went down. His head bounced off the hot pavement. His concussion probably did more damage than I had but I'd learned my lessons well. I threw myself on top of him, pinning his wrists to the ground. Baker outweighed me by at least sixty pounds. I had to finish him before he recovered.

As a fourth truck sped past us, I hooked my legs under his knees. With both hands on his wrists, I only had one weapon left in my arsenal. I reared up and drove my forehead into Baker's nose.

I'd hoped to knock him unconscious but I didn't have enough weight and power for that. No matter. He cried out in pain and his grip on his pistol loosened. I scrabbled for the weapon, ramming my knee up into his chin as I grasped for it.

Panting, I trained the pistol at his bloody face. "Officer Baker. You're demoted. You're just Michael Baker now. How does that feel?"

My knees were bruised and blood dripped from my face. I wasn't sure how much of the blood belonged to Baker. From the way my forehead felt, I guessed some of it was mine. I'd aimed for a hit square on his nose but I must have caught a ridge of bone around his deep-set eyes.

Shaking, I got to my feet and backed away, leaning on the car that had nearly knocked us both dead. I glanced back to see the trucks parked alongside each of the armory's loading docks.

"Drop that weapon!" I looked up. It was Lt. Stevenson. As the trucks rammed through Gate 12's maw, he'd climbed back to his post atop the parapet. His rifle was trained on me.

I shrugged and tossed the weapon away.

As Baker glared at me, one of his eyes had already begun to fill with blood. Coughing and still gasping in pain, he managed a thin smile.

Evelyn stepped out of the shack and strode toward me. Then she turned, walking backward, addressing the crowd beyond the gate. "I've got one of your spies here! Turn around and go home or I'll make an example of her!"

A lone voice called back, "We have no home!"

Evelyn scanned the crowd, searching for the woman who dared to reply. "Tanya? Is that you?"

A young blonde pushed her way to the front. It was the woman I'd replaced as Eye's nanny. She carried the American flag on a short pole. The flag was upside down, the symbol of the nation in distress. I broke into a grin at the sight. I'd known her all my life, but never as a blonde, never by the name of Tanya Dunford.

"Stay outside the gate!" Evelyn yelled. "Stay out of the Circle or my men will open up on the crowd." She pointed to me. "And I'll make an example of your spy, right in front of all those children!"

The rebel did not budge. "They say what we have in common is we all love our children and want the best for them. That's not true for you, is it? You hate us, even the little kids."

"What do you think I am? A cartoon? I don't hate your children!" Evelyn snarled. "I just don't care about them as much as I do my own."

"Yeah, see ... that's kind of the same thing. You *are* a cartoon, Evelyn. If it helps you sleep at night — and it shouldn't — there are a lot of people like you. Also? Nobody likes you."

Tanya looked up at the men stationed on the parapet. "Is this your best? Is this what you imagined yourselves doing?"

"Remember Portland!" Evelyn screamed. "Do you climbers need another whipping?"

Evelyn pointed her pistol at Tanya. "Let you be the first, then."

I wasn't sure if Evelyn meant to shoot her or if it was just a threat. That question went unanswered. A ladder truck arrived. The driver began to angle toward the gate to cut off the entrance to the Circle.

That didn't matter. One by one in quick succession, each of the AUTONAVS parked next to the armory erupted. Balls of flame ripped up to the sky. The shockwave from the explosion blew me off my feet and bounced off the Circle's inner wall, making the roar of echoes worse.

I might have been hurt badly but I landed squarely on Michael Baker again. This time my right knee took his front teeth.

Operation Jericho was almost over. I suppose I should have felt sorry for Michael Baker. I didn't have it in me.

CHAPTER THIRTY-EIGHT

A column of black smoke poured into the sky from the burning building. As the flames ate through the Circle's ammunition stores, pops and smaller explosions sounded from the armory.

In the Bible, the walls of Jericho fell. On that afternoon of the full moon, New Atlanta kept its walls. Through clouds of dust and choking smoke, the Resistance stormed the Circle's gates instead.

Tanya led the way, waving her upside-down American flag. The elderly veterans followed her in, a slow, calm invasion. With the medals on their chests and berets on their heads, they strode in quiet dignity.

The civilians followed and, except for the excited cries of some children, the crowd was silent. It was if the parents did not yet dare believe that their desperate gambit had paid off.

The parrots in their perch did not fire into the crowd. I'd like to think they came to their senses, that it was a moral choice. Maybe they would have made another choice if they'd had access to more firepower.

My ears rang. Confused, I heard from the Circle's other invaders, a distant chant that grew closer, rising in defiance: "Don't hope! Do! Don't hope! Do!" As protesters poured in from Old Atlanta, New

Atlanta's streets rang and echoed with the battle cry of a volunteer army that carried no weapons. The voices of the weak and downtrodden joined for one powerful message. "Don't hope! Do! Don't hope! Do!"

The people marching into the square joined the distant chant. Maybe it wasn't such a bad motto, after all. I squeezed my eyes tight and asked, "Is this real?"

As I opened my eyes, Evelyn stumbled toward me. Her nose bled from both nostrils and her hair, usually piled high in an elaborate style, had fallen across her eyes.

"No," she said. "I will not allow this to be real."

I stiffened as she slipped behind me. She put her pistol's muzzle against my right temple. I felt so hot, the cool metal was almost a comfort.

Without Baker's gun or my parents' knives, I was hostage to Evelyn's whims and a few pounds of pressure on her trigger. I guess that had been true since we met.

"This is the Captain of the Guard! Everyone out or I shoot your spy!"

The veterans circled us and then formed a phalanx. Boxed in, Evelyn cast about nervously, searching for an ally or an exit.

"I mean it! I'll shoot her!"

Tanya pushed her way forward again. "And then what?"

"And then you, Tanya!" Evelyn said. There was new steel in her tone that made me believe her. "It must be Kill a Traitorous Nanny Day!"

Tanya gazed at us. She didn't seem intimidated in the least. "We aren't your nannies, anymore, Evelyn. We're soldiers fighting for a just cause."

Her courage gave me back my voice. "All soldiers know ours is a life of sacrifice. How many bullets you got, Evelyn?"

One of the vets spoke up, "*Oorah!*"

His compatriots answered, louder and as one, "*Oorah!*"

Compatriots is a good word. It means *fellow citizen*. I felt like I was one of them. For the first time, I felt like I mattered to someone besides my family. I was part of a larger family of strangers who stuck together because we believed we had value. We were commoners, yes, but our common experience unified us. That was our glue.

Moved, I wept silently. Some of the sudden emotion was fear my life was ending. I'd like to think that most of the surge of tears came from making some meaning for myself just in time.

A new voice rang out over the crowd, long and loud. "The Circle ... is broken!"

The dust had begun to settle and a tall figure climbed atop the ladder truck. It was my Resistance contact from my first night in Atlanta. Dressed in camo fatigues, Chantelle still wore a huge wig and big dangly hoop earrings. She looked almost dainty as she took a moment to balance herself.

Using a bullhorn, Chantelle gave her first order, "All AWE and CSS troops, stand down! If you put your weapons down and leave now, I can guarantee your safety but you have to do it within the next twenty seconds."

"Or what?" Evelyn shouted at her.

"Or the war is still on and you lose, Captain." Chantelle's tone was calm and reasonable, as if she were asking a small child to hand over a favorite toy. "Put your weapon down. Only a savage keeps fighting after the war is lost."

The radio on Evelyn's belt came alive. "Brody to Captain Rossi. Come in, please. Urgent!"

Evelyn brought the mic to her lips. "Go ahead."

"Ma'am, the hack just put out a new alert. It's going to the hospital. They made it look like it's coming from us again."

"What's it say, Brody?"

"It's an alert to the emergency department to prepare to triage mass casualties, ma'am."

I yelled, "Enough!"

"Stand by," Evelyn told her officer.

"The girl's right," a man's voice called down from the parapet. Stevenson stood. The lieutenant nodded to his men and they joined him in placing their rifles on the deck. The parrots raised their empty hands above their heads and headed for the nearest ladder.

Evelyn's force had abandoned her. With her body pressed against my back, I felt the moment she gave up. As she sagged, I began to relax.

"Kismet, you asked me how many bullets I have. I guess I need only one." I turned as she placed the muzzle of her pistol under her jaw.

"Don't!" I said.

"Why not?"

"Eye."

"If I don't do it, you climbers will."

"You heard what the lady said. Put down your weapon and you get to live."

She hesitated. I grabbed the pistol so it could not fire and gave a sharp twist. Evelyn still held the weapon but it was no longer pointed at her head. The muzzle was pointed to the sky.

"Don't be stupid. You've got a daughter and, for God's sake, you're still rich! Complaining when your belly's full is *such* bad form. I know how you feel about bad form."

"You could never understand. It's not about the money — "

"It's about power. You'll still have your castle and fabulous advantages most will never dream of, but you might have to settle for half."

"That's what you don't get, Kismet. People like me attain our position for a reason. We can't be satisfied with half a loaf. We are ... we are never satisfied."

"Learn. Most people would burn all their money if they had yours, Evelyn. Grow up."

"This isn't how you're supposed to talk to a suicidal person, Kismet."

"You aren't suicidal, Evelyn. You're only feeling what the rest of us feel all the time."

A tear slipped down her cheek. "Pathetic and self-pitying?"

"Nah. Just powerless. Look around. Nobody here has money. We just want to eat and maybe get some control over our lives."

I recognized the look in Evelyn's eyes. I'd seen that same look on Clayton Dobbs' face as I threw a rope over a high tree branch and placed the noose around his neck. We offered Dobbs a chance to speak his final words but he refused. The neighbor who'd stolen desperately needed rations from the people of Campbellford never apologized. I didn't detect a hint of anger or fear before the rope went taut. Dobbs simply went to his doom resigned to his fate, as if his death was nothing more than the erasure of a mistake.

For Eye's sake and for the fate of Atlanta, I hoped for better of Evelyn.

"I've feared you and I've hated you," I told her. "I even felt a little sorry for you. Now? Now I'm just embarrassed for you. You can do and be so much better. You were one of us once. Remember how that felt?"

Tanya came forward. "You really do inspire a mix of emotions on the negative end of the spectrum, Evelyn!"

"Don't step on my moment, Sissy."

"Right. Sorry."

Confused, Evelyn looked back and forth at us. "Sissy? Not … not Tanya?"

I always looked like Mama. My sister got Daddy's square jaw. "You didn't let just one spy into your home. You let in two. Allow me to introduce my sister, Susan Beatriz."

"I joined the military to be a citizen and to train to be a doctor," Susan said. "I was assigned to Intelligence instead so I had to find another way to save lives."

"In fairness, they did place you where you had the aptitude," I added.

At that moment, a helicopter gunship rose over the rooftops, circled us twice and hovered at the edge of the square in perfect firing position. All eyes shifted to the war machine and a message shivered through the crowd like an urgent wind. Over the clatter of the gunship's blades, I heard the words, "stand your ground," and "last resort."

Grammy barely spoke of the massacre in Campbellford and never visited the ditch. However, as I stared up at that hunter-killer helicopter armed with missiles and machine guns, the one thing she did say about the mass murder came back to me. "If they're willing to do that to refugees, someday they'll come for us."

My sister waved her flag in a frantic circle. I thought she was signaling the pilot to refrain from killing us all. That wasn't it. The signal was known only to second-class citizens. One by one at first, and then in groups, the crowd turned toward the gunship. Everyone, even the children, raised their arms straight out to each side, even with their shoulders. With open palms and standing with their feet together, the image was as unmistakable as it was indelible. They did not mock the crucifixion, but they did succeed in clearly mimicking the iconic pose.

We could have dashed for the yawning gate. However, retreat would mean we'd never advance. The Resistance stood against the might of the Select Few. We were as trees in the forest, ready to be cut down for the cause. Surrender would get us no further than failure.

My parents had been experts in combat techniques. Daddy and Mama taught me how to fight. Until that moment, I had failed to understand the depth of gallantry in an act of radical pacifism. Peaceful resistance required more bravery than charging in with a gun.

"We have more people than you have bullets," I said. "We showed you mercy, Evelyn, but be warned, more of us are coming. And, as you can see, we aren't leaving."

Evelyn gasped, her jaw slack. "How is this possible?"

"This is how far the Select Few have pushed us down," I told Evelyn. "No place to go but up or dead. Be gracious in defeat. Stand down."

She shook her head. "Greater love hath no man..."

"Evelyn?"

Slowly, she raised the radio mic to her lips. "This is the Captain of the Guard. This will be my final order. Zeta Zulu. Acknowledge."

A moment passed and the reply came, "Repeat?"

"Zeta Zulu. Rossi, out."

"What's that?" I asked.

"Z is the end of the alphabet and Zeta Zulu is code for our last resort: surrender."

I wasn't certain I should believe her until the helicopter gunship wheeled around. It abruptly buzzed away to the south like a giant metal dragonfly.

It was as if we were all holding our breath. Relieved, there was a brief moment of silence. So prepared for death were we, we couldn't trust that we'd been spared. When the realization of our victory hit, it came all at once. We were still hugging and cheering as more newcomers from Old Atlanta arrived to join our ranks.

I turned to Evelyn. "You are relieved of duty, Captain."

She gave a slight nod. No longer a predator at the top of the food chain, her eyes dulled.

Slowly and gently, I pulled the pistol and the radio from her hands. I raised the radio mic to my lips. "Brody, this is the Resistance. Tell the hospital to expect a mass influx to triage. New Atlanta has fallen and it is ours. No gunshot wounds. Casualties have been avoided."

Turning to the crowd, I yelled, "New Atlanta is just Atlanta again! Welcome home!"

Amid the mass celebration, my sister rushed to embrace me.

"Hi, Sissy."

"You know I hate that."

"After all this, I guess I will have to start calling you Susan. Despite the blonde hair, you look more like a Susan than a Tanya."

Evelyn seemed smaller. She stared at my sister. "How is it possible *you* snuck in?"

"You said it yourself," I said. "Biometric records can be faked."

"It was AWE that got me in touch with the hackers," Susan explained. "They made the breach possible. So ... thanks, I guess."

Evelyn said nothing more and wandered away in a daze.

Surrounded by the cheering crowd, Susan hugged me again. "Winning was such a long shot, kind of restores your faith in God, doesn't it?"

"Nah, I'm still a heathen," I admitted, "but my faith in people just got a big boost."

CHAPTER THIRTY-NINE

"Sorry to take your job," I told Susan.

"I was recon. You delivered the tip of the spear. That was the job. You were the only one I could trust."

"Changing biometric records to match your face can't be easy."

"Took a huge bribe from disreputable people. Cost was a factor, sure."

"So you're saying I got the job because I was available?"

"That's how a lot of people get their jobs, Kismet."

"I almost didn't make it."

"I know. Sorry about Josh and Nash."

I looked at her, mystified.

"The guys who beat you up. I knew Evelyn would take it as a personal affront if her own maid got a black eye inside the Circle. A matter of pride."

"Uh ... I guess this is where I'm supposed to say thank you, right?"

"That was the moment," she said, "but I won't blame you if you let it slip by."

"Did the men who beat me up and the woman impersonating an AWE guard get away?"

"That woman was a real guard, a sympathizer to the cause. There are many, especially after their benefits got cut. Those in charge always seemed to act as if loyalty was a one-way street. Today they finally found out otherwise."

"But what happened with my attackers?"

"Attackers? Don't be dramatic. Josh and Nash gave you a bruise and never left the Circle. They've been holed up in a sub-basement in Mechanicsville. If it were that easy to pass in and out of the gates, we wouldn't have needed you to bring in the hack chip."

"When I see those guys, I'll be sure to thank them with a kick in the ribs."

We laughed but she sobered quickly. "Chantelle wants to see you." Susan glanced over her shoulder. "You'll have to get in line, though. She's got a lot of orders to sling. Taking New Atlanta was easy compared to the challenge of keeping it. There are immense resources here. We have to inventory them, ration them and figure out how we're going to keep the good juju going. Help me follow through on that. After getting a bruised cheek, you don't want the broken Circle to be in vain, do you?"

"So I've got another job?"

"First order of business is to fix all the gates."

"So they can all shut?"

Susan shook her head and smiled. "So they stay open, permanently. New moon's comin'. New day for the Circle, too."

Our greatest fear in the weeks that followed was that the billionaires would abandon the Circle. Chantelle forbade anyone taking hostages from the Select Few. That was a gamble. We worried that if all the billionaires left we'd be open to a punishment similar to that of Portland.

Our fears were unfounded. As Atlanta was made whole again, people could come and go as they pleased. Refugees were welcome within the Circle and many found homes there. The billionaires were still billionaires so most of the Select Few had little impetus to flee.

The new provisional government declared of the transition, "The fall of New Atlanta is not a revolution. It is a return to the norms that made America great. We will all live and work together for a better tomorrow. We do not hope. We do. What we do is take care of each other. It's called society. Our society *will* be great again."

However, one family decided to act on their contingency plans. The Rossis would flee to their acreage in Alaska. Despite Chantelle's assurances that they were in no danger, Evelyn insisted they had to evacuate.

Wanda, Susan and I escorted the Rossi family to their helipad. Evelyn wore a brave face and spoke at length of the great future that awaited them in Alaska. Kirk remained mostly silent, grunting in forced agreement.

Evelyn crossed her arms and looked me up and down. "I see you have your knives back."

"They were a gift. Just having them with me makes me feel better."

She pointed at my hip. "And your new sidearm? Stolen from my nightstand?"

"Confiscated," I said. "For the cause."

"I guess this is where we say goodbye."

I held out my hand. "Evelyn Rossi, a person of means among the blessed."

Grudgingly, she took my hand in hers and shook. "Kismet Beatriz, a person of substance."

Eye was happy to have both her nannies' attention, if only for a short time. She was also excited to see more of the world outside the Circle. "At the farm in Alaska, there are no walls. Mother says distance will do!"

Wanda leaned on Susan and me to lower herself to her knees to give Eye a long embrace. The pair whispered to each other for a while before the child kissed the old woman on the cheek. Both shed tears. They knew this would be the last time they saw each other.

Eye hugged Susan and me and rushed to get into the transport. As the helicopter blades whirred and began to gather speed, Kirk Rossi helped Wanda to her feet. He'd known his servant longer than he'd known his own mother. He gave her a firm handshake and said, "Good-bye, Wanda."

Straining her voice above the din of the helicopter blades, I heard her say, "Juanita! My name is Juanita! I'm taking over your house and a refugee family is moving in! They're originally from Mexico! Two girls, three boys, and the parents are women! They're both mechanical engineers!"

Kirk Rossi had a weak heart. By the way he paled at this news, I wondered if Juanita was saying goodbye or trying to kill him.

"Goodbye!" I told Evelyn. "No hard feelings."

She sneered at me as she climbed aboard the helicopter.

"I think she might still have some hard feelings," Susan observed dryly.

I smiled. "That's a shame. We weren't so different. She used to be a climber. She forgot what being outside the Circle was like," I replied.

"Bull!" Juanita said as we waved to Eye. "Evelyn forgot how to be kind, if she ever knew."

As we walked down the ramp from the Rossis' helipad into the arboretum, we found residents enjoying the Circle's park, picnicking along the man-made stream. The water looked crystal clear and inviting.

"Turns out there really was enough for everybody," Susan said. "We're all Utopians now."

Juanita caught my look. "What's the matter, Kismet? Underwear bunched up? Sneakers in a twist?"

"I don't know. It's just ... Evelyn was Captain of the Guard. Now she's flying off to New York, then Alaska. She still has her husband and Eye — "

"And billions," Susan added.

"Yeah! Doesn't it feel like we let the bad guys get away?"

Juanita shook her head. "If we'd pulled a French Revolution number on the Select Few and sharpened our guillotine blades, the war would have kept going. We would have lost the war for hearts and minds."

"Evelyn lost her post but other than that, she's still got it all," my sister giggled. "Hell, I'd marry a billionaire megalomaniac with a weak heart any day!"

"Not funny, Susan," I said.

"Kinda funny."

"Why are you the way you are?"

"Same as you, bad childhood."

Juanita was not amused. "By showing mercy, we avoided becoming like them. I've lived with the Rossi family all my life. They thought of themselves as the pinnacles of the species, role models for the rest of us peons. You know the origin of the word peon, right? Pee on? To me, the Select Few are a terrible warning of how not to act. To be a human being, you don't have to push everyone else down to prove your worth. Kirk was always too much like his father, too concerned with who was doing well, never wondering about who was doing the world any good. There's a lot of hard road between doing well and doing good."

"Maybe so," I said, "but Evelyn will sleep on clean sheets for the rest of her life."

"She didn't win," Juanita insisted. "I know my little girl. Eye is the future. She'll rise. She may even become the queen of Alaska for all I know. I brought Eye up to be clever and to know the difference between right and wrong. She has what her mother never had. My girl won't forget how good kindness feels."

I wished I were not so skeptical. "You think it'll stick?"

"She and I had a secret from when she was seven. I told her she was called Eye because she sees the way things are and how they should be. She'll have the power to make things right. I predict that if she decides to have children, she won't let Evelyn near them without supervision. She knows me so she knows who her mother and father are."

As we exited the arboretum, my sister and I parted ways with Juanita. We walked in silence toward our new home. Lisa and Buddy would be waiting with Grammy. When we brought her to Atlanta, my grandmother often called Lisa by my name. Lisa's presence was a comfort to Grammy when our duties called us elsewhere. Grammy loved her new home, her new rooftop garden and, most of all, air conditioning.

I should have been happy but I was still overwhelmed.

Reading my mood, Susan asked if I was okay.

"Sure. Just a lot to do to make the Circle work. We've got at least some CSS on our side. The way veterans get treated, it was inevitable some would join the rebellion."

"We're taking it back to the way things were. We'll be fine. Cooperating is good business for the Select. They've got too much invested here to leave."

I wanted to believe her. "I wish I had your confidence. How did you know things were going to work out?"

"It's not like it was foretold in a prophecy or anything. For me, it was always simpler than that. The Select Few always claimed to be better at math. They weren't."

"How do you figure?"

"Simple. They are the Select Few. We are many. The numbers were always on our side. Grammy would say that we all just had to row in the same direction."

"'We are many.' Maybe that should be our new motto."

I have looked back on the day the Circle's armory exploded many times. When I ponder that memory, the mixture of pain, terror, elation and sudden deafness ... it's all there, as fresh as yesterday. I remember the blinding brightness of the flames, visible even as I squeezed my eyes shut. The sudden wall of heat that followed the wave of sound felt like candles burning an inch from my skin. The smell of accelerant penetrated New Atlanta for weeks after the explosion.

As I stir these indelible recollections of the most important moment of my life, I don't like myself. I like to think we redeemed ourselves. I allowed myself to feel the thrill of victory without becoming Evelyn. But I hated her and the Select Few so much, I see now how easy it would be to become like her. I don't hate her anymore. I pity her, which is the one thing that would anger her most.

It was only after we allowed Evelyn and Kirk to go free that I understood the true mission of the Resistance. We weren't trying to break the Circle. We were raising up anyone who needed help.

The Select Few told us that helping people was too hard. They wanted us to believe life was unfair and that was the natural order.

They weren't altogether wrong. Life is not fair. However, it is up to us to try to make it that way.

Sometimes I still squeeze my eyes tight and ask aloud, "Is this real?" When reality falls short of our dreams, we work together to make it real, to make things right. Just as we suspected all along, there was enough for everyone.

Don't hope. Do. We are many.

AFTERWORD

"I don't try to describe the future.
I try to prevent it."
~ Ray Bradbury

Thank you for reading *Citizen Second Class*. Authors and their books live and die by reviews. If you enjoyed this novel, please leave a review wherever you purchased it.

~

We are many. Are you one of us? If so, you're invited to check out the author's note through the *Citizen Second Class* tab and the merch at AllThatChazz.com.

Life is not fair. Make it that way.

~ RCC

IF YOU ENJOY APOCALYPTIC FICTION...

Amid Mortal Words

A dangerous stranger met on a train leaves behind a powerful book.
With mere words, this book could destroy the world or save it. This
power is now in the hands of one man relying on a mysterious woman
to guide him toward the Apocalypse or away from our destruction. It's
a roller coaster ride filled with twists and turns toward a surprising
conclusion that will keep you up all night reading.

This Plague of Days

What will you do to protect your family in the zombie apocalypse?
Young Jaimie Spencer is an unlikely hero amid the ashes and ruins of
our world. On the spectrum and selectively mute, he's more obsessed
with his dictionary than with the fate of humanity. However, before
this epic story is over, Good will do battle with Evil and Jaimie is our
champion.

Robert's most successful series to date, *This Plague of Days* won

Honorable Mention in their Self-published Ebook Awards from *Writers' Digest*.

All three seasons of this trilogy are available as an omnibus or individually as ebooks or paperbacks on Amazon.

AFTER Life

Zombies will soon invade the United States. Which side will you join, the infected or the damned?

Artificial Facilitation Therapy for Enhanced Response (AFTER), was a biomimetic stem cell nanotechnology with numerous health and wellness applications. Then a military contractor weaponized it using brain parasites. When the zombie apocalypse we soon discover that genetically engineered zombies are hard to kill.

Officer Daniel Harmon is tasked with stopping the epidemic. Dr. Chloe Robinson needs to get her creation back under control. We can't always get what we want.

The *AFTER Life* trilogy is available now on Amazon as ebooks or in paperback.

Robot Planet

The robots are unfailingly polite until the moment they kill you. This future isn't merely a forbidding dystopia. It's cyberpunk scary.

In this series of four novellas, three very different people join forces to combat the rise of the Next Intelligence. The odds are against us.

Start your next adventure by grabbing *Robot Planet, The Complete Series*, available at Amazon in paperback or ebook.

Haunting Lessons

This is not a ghost story. It only begins that way.

Tamara is a young woman from the Midwest who experiences an unspeakable tragedy. Soon she sees apparitions. That's only the beginning of her adventures. Running away to New York, she soon discovers a secret world of dark magic doing combat with alien forces from another dimension.
If she is to save the world from the coming invasion, Tam must train to become a leader among the Choir Invisible. She fights for us all.

Death Lessons, *Fierce Lessons* and *Dream's Dark Flight* are also part of this series of gripping adventures.

All Empires Fall

How will the world end?

In this short story collection, Robert shares several tales of the apocalypse. It comes in flood and fire. It stabs at us out of the darkness of space.

Robert Chazz Chute many dark ideas for you to consider and revel in as you stay up through the night turning pages to each ending of our world.

ALL BOOKS BY ROBERT CHAZZ CHUTE

~ DYSTOPIAN AND APOCALYPTIC FICTION ~

THE AFTER Life TRILOGY

INFERNO

PURGATORY

PARADISE

AFTER Life (Box Set)

* * *

Amid Mortal Words

* * *

This Plague of Days, Season 1

This Plague of Days, Season 2

This Plague of Days, Season 3

This Plague of Days, Omnibus Edition

* * *

Robot Planet, The Complete Series

* * *

Haunting Lessons, Book 1 of The Dimension War

Death Lessons, Book 2 of The Dimension War

Fierce Lessons, Book 3 of The Dimension War

Dream's Dark Flight, Book 4 of The Dimension War

~ TIME TRAVEL ~

Wallflower

~ CRIME THRILLERS ~

The Night Man

Brooklyn in the Mean Time

Bigger Than Jesus, Book 1 of The Hit Man Series

Higher Than Jesus, Book 2 of the Hit Man Series

Hollywood Jesus, Book 3 of the Hit Man Series

The Divine Assassin's Playbook (Hit Man 1 - 3)

Resurrection, A Hit Man Novel

~ COLLECTIONS ~

Murders Among Dead Trees

Sometime Soon, Somewhere Close

Self-help for Stoners

All Empires Fall

* * *

~ NON-FICTION ~

Do the Thing: The Last Stress-busting Book You'll Ever Need

ABOUT THE AUTHOR

Robert Chazz Chute is a former journalist and winner of eight writing awards. He writes apocalyptic epics and killer crime thrillers from Other London.

Find out more at AllThatChazz.com.

For inquiries, contact:
expartepress@gmail.com

For daily updates and behind-the-scenes peeks, join the Fans of Robert Chazz Chute Facebook page.

www.ingramcontent.com/pod-product-compliance
Lightning Source LLC
Chambersburg PA
CBHW031223260626
47169CB00007B/2172